Quest Chasers
THE DEADLY CAVERN

Quest Chasers
THE DEADLY CAVERN

Grace and Thomas Lockhaven

Edited by David Aretha

TWISTED KEY
publishing

2016

First Printing: 2016

ISBN 978-1-365-60988-6

Twisted Key Publishing, LLC
405 Waltham Street Suite 116
Lexington, MA 02421

www.twistedkeypublishing.com

Ordering Information:
Special discounts are available on quantity purchases by corporations, associations, educators, and others. For details, contact the publisher at the above listed address.

U.S. trade bookstores and wholesalers: Please contact Twisted Key Publishing, LLC by email twistedkeypublishing@gmail.com.

"Keep writing, one day I'll be reading your mysteries." Mr. Ownby, my 5th grade English teacher, you will never know how powerful and exciting those words were to a hyperactive over creative young man. You instilled in me a work ethic at an early age and encouraged me daily to write and improve. Thank you.

Thomas Lockhaven

Stephen, this book wouldn't exist if it weren't for you. I'm very grateful for all your support, for helping me in every way you could. You have brought me lots of joy and showed me to always be happy and have fun. I'm eternally thankful and always think of you when I reread this story.

Grace Lockhaven

Contents

Acknowledgements

We would like to thank David Aretha, our editor, for his patience and excellent guidance. His guidance was invaluable.

Special thanks to Jelev for his artistic imagination.

Grace and Thomas Lockhaven

Faceplant

Mrs. Keystone's class had never been so quiet. In front of the class stood Drew Morris. All eyes stared transfixed as he gesticulated wildly as if trapped in the world's largest invisible spider web. Each of his classmates leaned forward in their desks, not wanting to miss a single word...

"This tree, it was different than all the other trees. It was gnarled and twisted and it was like it was alive!"

Drew's eyes opened wider than one would think humanly possible when he said the word *alive*. Sara Williams, actress and star of many Swift Creek Middle School theatrical performances, raised a shaky hand to her head, let out an audible gasp, and swooned.

Drew, caught up in the moment, paused for effect and whispered.

"I'm not sure why," he said, shaking his head, "but I walked closer to the tree. When I was just a few steps from it, the ground started shaking and then suddenly the roots ripped out of the ground like big, giant hands and they wrapped around me." Drew slapped his hands together as he entwined his fingers like a meat sandwich, prompting the students in the front row to jerk their heads back. His face turned red, and his hands trembled as he squeezed them together as tightly as possible.

"Drew…Drew…." He was about to go into the part about how he escaped when his teacher's voice finally broke through. "Drew!!!"

Drew looked up inquisitively at Mrs. Keystone, his English teacher, slightly annoyed at interruption.

"Drew." She spoke kindly and calmly. "You were supposed to tell a story about the most exciting thing that has ever happened to you. This wasn't a creative writing piece. Your story…"

Drew interrupted. He could immediately feel his round face growing red, his ears burning. "Mrs. Keystone, this *is* a true story! This really happened!"

The entire classroom erupted with laughter. Drew shrank back in embarrassed anger. "It's true," he said, his voice raising to a shriek. "It happened just two days ago, I'm not a liar!"

This only made everyone laugh harder.

"Drew," said Mrs. Keystone as she gently placed her hand on his trembling shoulders, "please take a seat. We'll talk after class."

Drew nodded and turned toward his desk—then ever so elegantly tripped over Sara Williams's bedazzled pink and silver converse and face-planted with a sickening thud onto the tile floor.

His lip quivered as the last bit of oxygen escaped his lips with an "ughhh." *This floor is incredibly cool.*

The sound of laughter rang in his ears. "Epic," yelled one of his classmates.

Drew felt a strong hand grab his own. He looked up into the face of Tommy Prescott.

Tommy smiled at him as he helped him to his feet. "Impressive face-plant; stunt work may be in your future," said Tommy, arching his eyebrows matter-of-factly.

Drew cautiously climbed into his desk; he had had enough attention to last a lifetime.

Bristling with anger, Mrs. Keystone slammed her hand onto her metal desk. "Everyone be quiet," she said, emphasizing each word.

Mrs. Keystone was a petite woman with kind eyes, but when the corners of her lips curled downward toward her chin, she looked like a giant—a giant that meant business. "I would have expected a little more understanding from you. Obviously, Drew misunderstood the project, and he, might I add, presented an excellent story."

She stood perfectly still, except for her head, which smoothly swiveled like a radar dish from one side of the classroom to the other. She made sure that she met every student's eyes before returning her attention back to Drew.

Her face softened when she spoke.

"Drew," she spoke kindly. "I will expect a new *actual story* from you tomorrow."

Drew wished that he could melt right into the seat of his desk. His neck prickled as he felt every single eye upon him, judging him. Feeling defeated and angry, he nodded his head.

"Yes, Mrs. Keystone." He could barely whisper her name.

Drew sat quietly, his breathing shallow, his heart pounding. He wanted to cry; he wanted to tell the entire class that they were all jerks.

I'm an idiot—what did I think would happen? How could he blame them for laughing? *I would have laughed too. But it* did *happen; I still have the scrapes and bruises all over my body.* He slowly pushed up his shirtsleeve, revealing an arm covered in scrapes and bruises.

As Drew sat tormenting himself, he suddenly became aware of a folded slip of notebook paper sliding across his desk.

Great, the harassment continues…. What's next? Facebook, Instagram?

Drew envisioned how it would play out. Pictures of him totally engrossed in his tree story with hashtags like #DrewsAnIdiot, #DrewsMagicalTree, #ExtremeTreeHugger, #FacePlanting101.

His life was over. Suddenly homeschooling seemed like his only option to gracefully live out the rest of his middle school and high school years. *Do they have homeschooling for college?*

Carefully he unfolded the paper behind his English book so Mrs. Keystone didn't see.

On the page, there was a very simple handwritten note.

Drew, you are incredibly brave. We believe you! Meet us by Walter's statue after school. Eevie and Tommy.

Drew didn't turn around. In fact, he still felt doubtful that Eevie and Tommy believed him. He liked Eevie—she was incredibly smart and friendly and her eyes were like liquid sunshine. He thought about that for a moment, Eevie gazing…. But then there was Tommy. He didn't really know Tommy too well, but he seemed nice enough. He knew one thing for sure, though: Eevie and Tommy were inseparable.

Swift Creek Middle School had installed a new electronic tone system to denote the beginning and ending of classes. Instead of the clanging of a bell, there was a "tonal beep" that was supposed to enkindle calmness throughout the student body. Psychologists had figured that this soft tone gently persuaded the student body to move peacefully en masse from class to class. The final tone released the beasts into the wild.

The tone theory seemed to work well except for the final departure, where students stampeded out of the school like wildebeests in a National Geographic special. Drew, not wanting to be a part of the pack, surreptitiously slipped out the classroom. He darted through the art department and out the back of the school. Cautiously, he made his way to the corner of the school facing the parking lot.

Peering around the corner of the main building, he patiently waited a good five minutes until most of the students had boarded their buses or been picked up by their parents. He wanted to avoid further public humiliation at all cost. Head hung low, he tried to walk as inconspicuously as possible to the now almost empty bike rack.

Drew pulled his hoodie over his head and looked up at the statue of Walter Emery, founder of Swift Creek Middle School. Walter was a foreboding figure, and in every picture Drew had seen of the man, he looked as if he was bloated and suffering from horrible gas.

Even now, Drew felt as if Walter was staring down at him with a look of disdain, like someone had put a hot herring in his cummerbund, a crime for which there was no acquittal. Drew looked up to the afternoon sky. The gray and black clouds were in a heated argument, threatening to pour down on him at any second.

"Drew! Drew!"

Drew jumped and cautiously peered out from the shelter of his hoodie. His classmate, Eevie, waved to him. He swallowed hard as she and Tommy Prescott approached.

"I never stared at her in class," he blathered, looking from Eevie to Tommy as if pleading for his life, afraid that Tommy would know that the song "All of Me" by John Legend played in his head every time he looked at Eevie.

As Eevie drew closer, she gave him a reassuring smile. "What did you say?"

"Nothing," mumbled Drew, when he realized he wasn't about to become Tommy's personal tackle dummy.

"Tough crowd in there," she said, punching his shoulder playfully. *I'll never wash that shoulder again,* thought Drew to himself.

Eevie Davenport had shoulder-length brown hair and brown eyes with golden specks that sparkled in the sunlight. Her cheeks glowed red from the cold October breeze. Eevie was extremely kind to everyone and easy to like. She was a modern-day renaissance girl, incredibly smart and giving; she mentored other students if they began falling behind or even just needed some encouragement.

Everyone liked Eevie and instinctively, Drew knew he could trust her.

Then again, she was always accompanied by Tommy Prescott. Tommy was tall and athletic with blondish brown hair cut short. He had the face of certainty—that determined kind of face you see when you think of a soldier or an athlete. So Drew was surprised when Tommy said—

"Drew, it took a lot of courage to do what you did. I don't think I could have done that. You should be proud of yourself for standing up in front of everyone. Not many people would have done that."

Drew shook his head as a confused look crossed his face. He wanted to blurt out, *Yes, not everyone has the skillset to become a social pariah like me in a matter of minutes.*

But instead, he found himself saying, "You two believe me?"

He pulled his hoodie down off his head, his face matching the disbelief in his voice. The wind kicked up, tussling his curly red hair playfully. His hazel eyes narrowed as he searched their faces waiting for the joke where he was the punch line. "I basically told you that a tree grabbed me like an anaconda and tried to squeeze the life out of me, and you believe me?"

His eyes squinted, and he shook his head as if that would bring him back to reality, to a moment when Eevie was saying: "Hi, Drew. OK, this is what we call an intervention. Now my father is a child psychologist and…." His internal dialogue was interrupted by Eevie's angelic voice.

"We do. We believe you," said Eevie, her face breaking into a soothing smile. "I hadn't really thought about it for a long time, but you made me remember a story my grandfather told me—a story about a tree, a twisted tree like the one that you described…. I always thought he was just trying to scare us kids, but when you started talking about the tree, all those memories came back to me."

"The same thing happened to your grandfather?" asked Drew incredulously.

"Not quite the same thing," said Eevie smiling, "but he used to play in Black Hallow Park when he was a little boy."

Eevie leaned forward, the way that people do when they are about to tell something very interesting.

"He told me he went camping with a bunch of his friends. One of the older boys told a story about children mysteriously vanishing from the park. He, of course, thought that the older kid was just trying to scare him and his friends, but it frightened him so badly he couldn't sleep that night. He said when he got home he was exhausted, and his father asked him why he hadn't slept. Grandpa told him what the boys had said, and after that his father grew very silent. His dad's face turned really pale, and he told my grandfather: 'You are never to go into those woods.' He remembered his dad lowering his face to him, nose to nose, saying: 'Do you understand me? You are *not* to go back.'"

"OK," said Tommy, extending the *K* and moving his eyes from Drew to Eevie and then back to Drew.

He looked closely at Drew; he was transfixed by Eevie's story. *Was Drew even breathing?*

"Drew, Eevie, it's Tommy," he called out, waving his hand in front of their faces, "welcome back to what we like to call reality."

Eevie glared at him.

"I'm sorry," said Tommy apologetically. "I'm sure there is a rational explanation for all of this. Or, as they like to say on the National Geographic channel, a natural phenomenon."

Eevie ignored him and continued. "So here is where the story turns a little weird."

Tommy coughed and then pretended to be fascinated by the back of his hand. "I'm sorry, starts to get weird?"

Eevie continued, ignoring Tommy's comment. "He said a few days after he told his parents about the story, they had to travel to a funeral for a close friend of theirs. So his grandmother came to stay with him while they were gone. His dad had a study that he always kept locked, and while his grandmother was sleeping, he broke into his dad's office with a shoehorn."

"Pardon me, a what?" asked Tommy, a confused look on his face.

"A shoehorn. A metal thingy that you put on the back of your heel to help get your shoe on."

"OK, no idea. However, please continue."

Tommy arched his eyebrows and looked down at Drew. "Don't you even pretend like you know what the heck a shoehorn is."

Eevie shook her head in disbelief. "Just Google it. May I continue now?"

"Yes, please," smiled Tommy. Out of the corner of his eye, he could see Drew's thumbs busily searching "shoehorn" on his iPhone.

"So anyways, he said he went straight to the desk, but it was locked. He…"

Tommy looked up at the sky. "Eevie, can you give us the CliffsNotes version of the story? It looks like it's about to pour any second."

Eevie gasped and rolled her eyes skyward in exasperation. "Really?"

"Found it!" Drew proudly showed everyone a picture of a shoehorn on his iPhone.

"Oh, cool. I need one of those for my soccer shoes," said Tommy, staring at Drew's phone.

"Ugh," Eevie groaned. "Seriously? May I finish the story?"

"Sorry," whispered Drew. "Your grandpa was pretty smart—I would have never thought of that."

Tommy nodded in agreement. "Super smart. I honestly thought that it was a horn for your shoe. You know, like if the mall is really busy and you need to get through a crowd, you just honk your shoe horn."

"Drew! Tommy! You two are killing me. Do you want to hear the story or not?"

"Sorry," the boys said in unison, cowering under Eevie's admonishing gaze.

She shook her head and began again. "Here's the CliffsNotes version. He finally got the desk drawer open by prying it open with…." Exasperated, she looked at them knowing what was coming. "…the shoehorn."

She looked up surprised. "What, no comments from the peanut gallery?"

"No, we are riveted," Tommy, said. "Please continue."

"He said that when he was trying to pull the drawer open, he accidentally completely pulled it out of the desk, and underneath the drawer he found a thick envelope. He ripped that off and hid it in his pajamas. Now, this is where my grandpa's smarts make you guys look like a couple of rookies. He just managed to get the door shut when his grandma came around the corner."

"Oh, he is soooo dead," said Drew with a nod of his head.

"Nope, this is where my grandpa's *sneak gene* kicked in. He said he apologized to her and told her that he had a problem sleepwalking. He told her he had fallen down the stairs and acted like he had bruised his arm and twisted his ankle."

"Whoa, smart guy," said Drew, admiringly. "I would have probably just tried to stand really still like a statue, hoping that she was incredibly nearsighted."

"If you picked up a globe and took off your shirt, I'm pretty sure she would think you were Atlas," laughed Tommy.

"Seriously? Drew was almost killed by a tree, then the entire class thinks he had a psychotic episode, and you two are making jokes?"

"I was just trying to lighten the tension a little, Eevie. Geesh. Of course we're listening to you. I for one am spellbound." Tommy looked at Drew for support. "Go ahead, Eevie."

"My grandpa said he limped into the kitchen and had to wait for what seemed an eternity for his grandmother to make him some hot milk, which is supposedly a cure for sleepwalking. Finally, she went to bed."

"Sooooo…what was in the envelope?" whispered Drew.

"Inside there was a stack of newspaper clippings, each one describing the disappearance of numerous people at Black Hallow Park."

"So his friend wasn't lying," said Drew, suddenly excited.

"But," she said, pausing for dramatic effect, "there was one clipping that caught his eye. The person in one of the clippings had the same last name. The clipping was from September 14, 1942, and the person who had disappeared was his dad's twin brother. He never realized his father had a brother. No one ever spoke about him. He said he sat and stared at the picture in the article. His dad's brother had the same eyes, the same smile as his father."

Eevie looked at Drew. "Today is September 16th. You were attacked on the same day—seventy-five years later. That's really creepy...."

"Drew," said Eevie, excitedly, "this may be our chance to prove that you were telling the truth and find out what's really out there!"

"That sounds like a very bad idea," said Drew.

"What's out there is a *very* unhappy tree with some serious anger issues," said Tommy. "Most likely it wasn't nurtured as a sapling."

"Really," said Eevie, her voice filled with mock annoyance. "I don't think it was the *tree* that wasn't nurtured," she said smiling at

Tommy. "Drew, do you think you can show us where we can find the tree?"

"I can show you," said Drew, "but I'm not going near that tree again." He shook his head *no* as he spoke each word. "That tree nearly killed me!"

"Drew, we get it." Tommy raised his hands in an "it's OK, we understand" gesture. "We just want to know where the tree is, so we can do a little investigating on our own, and keep anyone else from danger if they happen to venture near that tree."

Drew's body gave an involuntary shiver as he thought about going back to the tree. "You guys are the only ones who believed me. Thank you…. I'll show you how to find the tree."

Tommy nodded with a smile. "Don't worry, you're in good hands."

Eevie put her hand on Drew's shoulder, her face becoming both determined and serious. "We're going to figure this out, together."

Drew smiled appreciatively. *Eevie has got to be the coolest girl I have ever met. I'll never wash this shoulder either.*

"Let's meet at my house at four," said Tommy. "If we go to the bus stop, we can get off at Evergreen and we won't have to worry about riding our bikes in the rain."

As if on cue, everyone looked skyward and watched as dark clouds raced like ghosts across the sky.

"OK," said Drew. "I'll be there."

Eevie nodded. "Sounds good."

BLACK HALLOW PARK, NOT SUCH A HAPPY PLACE...

The bus groaned to a stop, engulfing the trio in a swirling plume of noxious exhaust. It was still early enough in the afternoon that the bus was mostly empty except for a few passengers interspersed throughout. Drew, Eevie, and Tommy squeezed into a bus seat and braced themselves as the bus lurched forward. Black Hallow Park was only about a mile away, and it seemed as if they had only been on the bus for a few seconds when the air brakes hissed like a deflating balloon.

"That's us," said Tommy, jumping to his feet. "Let's go."

The park's entrance was surrounded by an old stone wall with a giant black wrought iron gate that read "Black Hallow Park:

Founded 1779." The park was immense with an area for camping, a nature museum with an auditorium, and a fully stocked lake with paddleboats and canoes where visitors could fish and swim. There were miles of paths that spread throughout the park like splayed fingers from a giant hand.

The clouds had been patient enough, and now a steady rain began to fall. Eevie and the boys pulled their hoods up as they walked past the old iron gate. The thick cloud covering meant that it would be dark soon.

"All right, Drew, let's find this tree before Eevie begins to complain about her hair."

Drew managed a weak smile, his mind was busy replaying the events of just a couple days ago. "He's just jealous, Eevie. We all know Tommy has the hair of a baby egret."

"I see how it is," Tommy said with a smile. "My hair believes in quality, not quantity."

The group wound their way deeper into the forest. The path grew darker and darker as the canopy of trees blocked the last bit of remaining light. Solitary drops of water fell around them, victors over the other raindrops that were captured by the dense canopy of leaves that loomed above them.

"Drew, are you sure you can remember the tree? It's getting crazy dark in here and they all…." Just then Tommy stopped talking.

Up ahead stood a magnificent tree. The trunk was twisted as if dozens of giant ropes had been coiled around each other. Unlike the other trees, there were very few leaves, and those that remained were a blackish brown color. Its branches erupted skyward like gnarled skeletal fingers. Roots like a jumble of veins and arteries surrounded the tree for what seemed like twenty feet or more. The tree was simply massive.

"Thaaaattt's the tree," whispered Drew, his hand shaking as he pointed.

Eevie drew in a sharp breath; her spine felt like it had turned to ice. Drew's fear was palpable. With trembling fingers, she pulled out her iPhone. "I'm going to GeoMark our location; it will tag where we are using a GPS app."

Tommy just nodded—hearing, but not really listening.

Next, Eevie clicked on the video button. The iPhone's electronic ding sounded alien in the stillness of the forest.

"What's the plan?" Drew's face was pale; cold sweat glistened on his forehead.

"We'll slowly approach the tree," Tommy said. "Make sure you stay *well* outside the reach of those roots. I think as long as we are together we'll be fine." Tommy sounded more sure than he actually was. Inside he could feel the blood rushing to his ears with every heartbeat.

As a group, they cautiously approached the tree, carefully stepping outside the intricate array of roots. Their eyes darted up and down, watching the tree and the roots for any movement. However, there was nothing, absolutely nothing. Just stillness.

Tommy relaxed a little. "Is this what they mean when they say the calm before the storm?"

"Heyyyyyy. What are you kids doing?!"

Drew screamed, falling to the ground, while Eevie and Tommy jumped and spun around, crouching low. Through the darkness of the night, they could just make out the silhouette of a man standing on the path behind them. His long, angular face was deeply shadowed under the brim of his hat, but they could still feel the intensity of his stare. Tommy reached down and helped Drew to his feet. He could feel Drew trembling.

"It's OK, Drew," Tommy whispered. "It's just the park ranger, he's…"

"The park is about to close." The ranger's voice took on a tone of suspicion cutting off Tommy mid-sentence. "What are you three doing out here in the woods in the dark?" The park ranger slowly played his flashlight across their faces, blinding them.

"We were just taking pictures of that beautiful old tree," said Eevie, her voice shaking slightly. "We were just about to leave."

"In the dark?" The ranger didn't wait for her answer. He stiffly walked past them toward the tree. Tommy noticed the ranger had a slight limp that gave his shadow a creepy jerk with each step.

"Sir, Eevie is telling the truth," Tommy explained. "Mrs. Keystone, our English teacher, asked everyone to do a report on a local legend. Eevie's grandfather told us that this tree...well, that it had supernatural powers. We don't really believe any of that; we just wanted to take some spooky pictures at night because we thought it would look creepier for our report. I'm sorry if we broke any park rules. We can just try to find some pictures online."

The ranger stared intently at Tommy and the rest of the group. He pulled his lips tight and nodded his head, then put his hand on the side of the giant tree. "This tree is over four hundred years old. It survived the devastating fire of 1856, when according to historical records, everything in this forest was burned down to the ground—yet somehow this tree survived. This tree has a lot of history. I'll give you a little tidbit about this tree that you can use in your report.... About five years ago, we gave a couple of historians permission to use ground-penetrating radar devices around the tree."

"Why would you use radar around the tree? Can't you just use a metal detector?" asked Eevie.

"Ground-penetrating radar allows you to visually see if there is anything below the surface without damaging the environment.

Metal detectors are great for finding buttons and knives and other types of artifacts, but you have to dig and they aren't always reliable."

"Did they find anything?" asked Tommy.

The ranger paused for a moment. "Yes. Yes, they did. They found a sword, a canteen, and two rifles twisted and buried in the roots. Curiously, there was no sign of a soldier's remains…"

Eevie stepped toward the ranger. "I'm confused. A lot of soldiers died here during the war. Why would they be surprised if there were no remains? Surely they would have buried him, or if he was injured, carried him to safety."

"Good question." The ranger turned the beam of his flashlight downward. In the shadows, the dark and twisty roots looked like serpents. "They found two bullets lodged in one of the roots. And the soldier's canteen had also been shot. You have to remember, most of these soldiers were poor farmers without a lot of food or weapons. They would not have taken the soldier and left his weapons behind; they were much too valuable. That's the mystery."

"Thank you, sir," said Tommy. "You've been a huge help."

"Thank you," whispered Drew, deep in thought.

The ranger glanced down at his watch. "I'll walk you kids out of the park. I wouldn't want anything to happen to you."

The small group walked in silence, each one playing and replaying the conversation over in their mind. The only sound was the rain splashing off the leaves and the occasional staticky burst from the ranger's walkie-talkie.

"Sir," asked Tommy, "if the legend were true about that tree...well, at least the ones where we've heard about people disappearing and such...why isn't the tree blocked off?"

The ranger paused. "Just because a tree survives a fire, and a soldier died cradled in its roots, doesn't mean it has some mysterious power. People make up stories to scare people, like Bigfoot or the Loch Ness monster. I've been a ranger here for thirty-seven years, and I haven't seen anything mysterious yet. People like to make something out of nothing."

Through the darkness, Tommy could see the outline of the ranger's house as they approached the gate. He wasn't sure why, but he always loved the way orange and yellow lights mixed and shined out from the windows at nighttime.

However, something wasn't right. Something stared back at him through the window, and then it was gone. It looked like a cat, but it didn't move like a cat. It moved like...

The ranger followed Tommy's eyes and looked back at Tommy.

"Oh...you have a cat," said Tommy, knowing that it wasn't a cat.

"Yes, I do," he smiled. "A black cat. Good night," said the ranger, still staring at Tommy—both of them knowing that he had seen something other than a cat...

The rest of the group seemed oblivious to the strange exchange between Tommy and the ranger.

"Good night," said the group in unison. The ranger closed the wrought iron gate behind them with a metallic clang. They continued walking toward the bus stop, the sound of a chain being put in place ebbing through the darkness.

When they had walked a few steps away, Tommy was about to tell them what he had seen, but Drew exploded. "The tree didn't do anything to him! He walked right up to it and basically petted it and NOTHING. You guys must think I'm crazy." He looked from Eevie's face to Tommy's face. "I'm not lying."

Eevie placed her hand on Drew's shoulder. "Listen, we believe you. You must have done something to make the tree try to devour you. I'm not sure what, though."

"Guys," said Tommy, "let's go. We can figure out everything on the bus."

The ride home was quite different; the bus was filled with weary travelers on the way home from work. Most of the passengers followed the universal norm, heads bowed staring at their cellphones as their thumbs danced about as if playing a miniature drum set.

The three children sat squished together on one seat, their heads close together, whispering so no one could hear them.

Tommy whispered, "Did you guys see the way the ranger looked at me when I mentioned the cat in his window? It was weird."

Eevie and Drew shook their heads "no" in unison.

"What do you mean?" asked Drew.

"I saw something in his window. It was black like a cat, but it didn't move like a cat. Then when I said something about it, he gave me a creepy stare. He knew I saw something, and he knows that I know it wasn't a cat."

"He's a ranger. It could have been a raccoon for all you know. He could be rehabilitating an animal. Who cares? In the grand scheme of things, who cares if he had an elephant in his house? We are dealing with a tree that has a history of turning people into Lunchables." Said Drew mystified.

"They are tasty," acknowledged Tommy. "Maybe I was just seeing things," said Tommy, trying to appease Drew. Inside, however, Tommy knew that "look." Something wasn't right, but he wasn't going to push the issue until he could speak with Eevie in private. "OK, let's get back to 'operation angry tree.'"

"Angry tree?" Drew inhaled and exhaled, shaking his head. *You're gonna be just fine.*

"Tonight is Friday night. Eevie, you can tell your parents we're going to go see a movie?"

"Sure," said Eevie, nodding. "Not a problem."

"What about me?" asked Drew, a worried look filling his face.

"Drew," smiled Tommy reassuringly, "you did everything you needed to do. Eevie and I will sneak into the park and shoot some video. Don't worry, we'll stay clear of the tree and the roots. You will be vindicated by my amazing videography—trust me, this tree will give everyone the creeps."

Drew looked at Tommy, his eyes filled with doubt.

"Are you doubting my videography skills or that Eevie and I will stay away from the tree? Trust me, we'll stay clear of the tree, the roots, the branches—we'll be fine!"

Just then, the bus hissed and screeched like an angry cat as it pulled to a stop at the intersection of Broad and Hamilton. The group disembarked and then huddled together on the sidewalk.

Eevie turned to Drew. "Remember, not a word of this to anybody. My folks will ground me until I'm forty if they find out!"

"I'm not gonna tell anybody. You have my word! Just please be careful. Don't try to do anything heroic on my behalf."

My Oversized Cranium

Eevie showed up at Tommy's door promptly at 7:30 p.m. She had just raised her hand to knock when Tommy swung open the door dressed in his best "going out" hoodie. Behind him, blue electric light flickered from the doorway of the living room. Tommy's parents had most likely settled in for a night of Netflix binge watching.

"Eevie's here. We're leaving now!" Tommy had to yell to be heard over the wall of sound blasting from the TV.

"Hi, Eevie! Have a good night! Be careful!"

"Hi, Mr. and Mrs. Prescott," said Eevie, arching forward onto her tiptoes, as if this would help project her voice.

"I always wondered which they really wanted me to have…a good night, or to be careful," Tommy said with a wink.

Eevie playfully pushed Tommy, shaking her head. "Tonight, I think we both know the answer to that."

"Sure you don't want me to drive you guys to the movies?" called out Tommy's dad.

"We're good—thanks, Dad!"

"Give me a call if it gets too bad and I'll come get you."

"Gets too bad? Eevie's mean to me at times, but it never gets that bad," laughed Tommy, raising his eyebrows. "See," said Tommy matter-of-factly, "even my parents know the truth."

"I mean the weather. We'd replace you with Eevie any day of the week," yelled his mother, laughing.

"My own mother. That's horrible." A look of mock disgust and anguish filled Tommy's eyes.

"Love you, honey. Call us if the *weather* gets too bad."

Eevie snickered and silently mouthed "honey."

"I'm their darling son, and your jealousy…well," paused Tommy, shaking his head, "it's just pitiful."

He turned his head and shouted into the doorway, "OK, will do!"

And with that, they were on their way.

Tommy reached down and retrieved his backpack that he had stashed in the boxwood bushes in front of his house.

"I know; you're impressed with my forethought," smiled Tommy.

"Actually, I am more impressed that you know the word *forethought*, and even more impressed that you actually used it correctly."

Tommy's hands flew to his chest, his face tilted skyward. "My heart. My heart…. You know it is possible to be engagingly smart and handsome." He turned his head expecting to see Eevie's eyes filled with remorse and acknowledging his immenseness; instead, she busied herself by putting on her helmet and climbing on her bike.

"My skillset is so underappreciated," said Tommy to no one.

The plan was pretty simple. Ride their bikes to the park without looking suspicious. Hide their bikes and then climb over the stone wall. Then, with their phones recording, they would try to make the tree come to life without getting killed. They weren't quite sure how to pull off that part of the plan, but they were sure they would come up with something. Tommy said something about taunting the tree, and Eevie of course used what she termed "selective hearing" and completely ignored him.

The ride to the park was uneventful. They had ditched their bikes across the street at the library. A mottled orange light shone through the park's gate, overwhelmed by the four huge spotlights illuminating a twenty-foot semicircle around the gate.

"Do you see what I'm seeing?" said Tommy, pointing toward the lights.

"That's not the only thing," whispered Eevie. "Look." She pointed toward the top corners of the gate. "Cameras."

"I'm sure Ranger Rick in there doesn't have a love life. He's probably sitting there staring at those cameras right now."

"We should have put a little more planning into this. The front of the gate is incredibly well lit; there's no way we won't be seen. Maybe we should just go back to your parents' house and work out a more thorough plan."

"Eevie, they have all of this protection at the gate because everyone goes in and out that gate." Tommy gestured at the gate as if this validated his statement. "You have to think outside the box; we can just climb the walls."

"Noooo way," said Eevie, shaking her head. "They are at least nine feet high, and while you are an amazing athlete—cough, cough—I don't have a standing or running four-foot vertical leap."

"No, neither do I. Thanks for the compliment, by the way. But we do have a ladder."

"You brought a ladder? Do you have *magic pockets* in those pants?"

Tommy paused. *No, but that would be way cool.* Instead he shook his head. "No, but I have a massive brain. It's why my parents told me that my head is so big." Tommy moved his hands in circles over the top of his head, emphasizing its largeness.

"They lied about one of those things," smirked Eevie.

"You really know how to hurt a guy when he is about to dazzle you with his creativity."

"It's a gift," replied Eevie, smiling.

"May I speak now?"

"I implore you, do go on. Please make manifest this ladder."

"Besmirch all you want. I know your true feelings."

Eevie shuddered, "I think I just threw up in my mouth. OK, get on with it. Show me your master plan."

"OK, the wall is nine feet tall. Not a song or the beginning of a poem—it's just a fact."

"Which you will traverse, with your mighty magic ladder."

"Was there a spelling quiz I missed out on or something? I'm trying to tell you how we will get over the wall."

"Sorry," smiled Eevie, "just nervous energy."

"It's fine," said Tommy, raising his hands. "OK, here's how we're going to do it. In my backpack I have a piece of rope and a knife. We have two bicycles that are each about four feet tall. We anchor them to the ground somehow, so they don't slide out from under us, and we tie them together. We'll need to find an area with some bushes in front of it to conceal the bikes. If we let the air out of the tires, they will be less likely to roll as well. If I can get you four feet up in the air, you should easily be able to pull yourself over the wall."

Eevie looked at Tommy, her lips curling downward. "I'm impressed."

Tommy bowed. "It all comes from my oversized cranium." Tommy carefully encircled his fingers in tiny orbits around his head, pointing again at its immenseness.

It took only a couple of minutes to grab their bikes and to find some bushes that would offer enough cover for them to build their makeshift ladder. Putting the bike ladder together, however, was a little more challenging. Even with the tires emptied, the bikes moved and rolled until Eevie had Tommy hold down the hand brakes as she tied them together. Tommy borrowed a couple of stakes surrounding a manhole cover that were pointed on one end and flat on top. He placed the bike against the wall, and then, placing a stake against the frame of the bike, he used his heel to stomp it firmly into the ground.

It certainly wasn't the sturdiest of ladders, but it would get them up and over the wall. Suddenly, everything became very, very real.

"You realize if we get caught," said Eevie, "we are going to be charged with trespassing and our parents are going to punish us for the rest of our lives."

"I know," said Tommy. "It felt really bad lying to my parents. But as far as we know, Eevie, this has been going on for hundreds of years. I've never felt more *right* about doing something in my life."

"Did you practice that?" asked Eevie, smiling nervously.

"I'm sorry, I cannot divulge my secrets of mock sincerity."

"I just wanted to make sure that you had thought it through and you didn't feel like it was something you *had* to do because you felt pressured to do it."

"No," smiled Tommy. "You aren't that good looking, especially not good looking enough for me to follow you into oblivion."

Yeah right, thought Eevie, and without another word, Eevie had climbed on top of the bikes.

"Remember," whispered Tommy, "when you get to the top, take your time—and then hang and drop on the other side. I'll be right behind you."

Tommy braced the bikes with his body as Eevie grasped the top of the wall. He grabbed her by the ankles, helping to push her up to the top.

Eevie felt the stone biting into her hands and she felt Tommy's hands carefully propelling her upward. Gasping and straining, she was able to throw one leg over the top. She sat motionless, catching her balance and her breath. Her heart was pounding in her chest. She knew that she literally and figuratively straddled the fence on going forward or turning back.

She turned to Tommy and nodded; she had made up her mind. Leaning forward and putting her weight on her forearms, she brought her other leg over the wall. The rough surface scraped into her wrists as she twisted to hang down the other side of the wall.

For a brief moment, she panicked and then let go, remembering to relax her body so her feet and ankles didn't take all of the impact. She hit the ground with an "oof" and rolled onto her side. She stared up at the wall. She was over. She could hear scraping on the wall; Tommy was on his way.

Tommy precariously stood, balancing on the seat of the bicycle. It wasn't as easy without someone holding it. Several times the bike lurched under his feet, and he was sure he was going to either smash into the wall or become one with the bush. He compressed his body as much as he felt safe and leapt upward, grasping for the top of the wall. It had begun to rain again, making his ascent much more difficult. From the other side of the wall, Eevie could see his fingers clawing into the stonework—she knew he must be ripping his fingertips to pieces, yet she was powerless to help him.

"Come on, Tommy," whispered Eevie urgently.

Tommy's feet slipped and slid across the stone wall as he tried to find just a small impression that he could wedge the toe of his shoe in. His hands were beginning to slip now and his feet kicked out to try to find the bike below him. Suddenly, his foot slid and stopped. With every bit of strength left in him, he pushed against his right foot and pulled upward with all his might. His chest landed awkwardly on the edge of the wall, knocking the wind out of his lungs.

He lay on top of the wall, gasping for breath. Down below, he saw Eevie staring up at him, her eyes filled with worry. Tommy threw a leg over the top of the wall, straddling it, and gave Eevie a shaky thumbs-up, letting her know everything was OK. Leaning onto his chest, he lowered himself until he was hanging against the wall. He dropped easily to the ground, and then managed to lose his balance on the wet grass, falling hard with a heavy thud onto his back.

"That was graceful," whispered Eevie.

"Thanks," gasped Tommy, trying to get air back into his lungs. "I think I injured my backpack."

Eevie smiled down at Tommy, shaking her head. "I take back the part about you being an athlete."

Eevie reached out her hand, pulling Tommy to his feet. Her face suddenly became serious. "I just realized we don't have a magic ladder on this side of the wall."

"We've got three hours before our parents check in on us. Don't worry," smiled Tommy, "I'll figure a way out."

Eevie nodded. "Alright, let's go."

Above, the moon fought valiantly to shine through the thick clouds. Small slivers of light impaled themselves into the ground, cutting through the dense forest like blades of light. Around them, trees stood like centurions, guarding whatever lay in wait for them deep in the forest.

"We should have made a map," Tommy said. "It's going to be difficult finding the tree in the dark. I can't even find my own hand, and I'm pretty sure it was on the end of my arm when I left home."

Eevie glanced at Tommy questioningly. "I geotagged the location on my phone, remember?"

"No. How?" asked Tommy, both confused and impressed.

Eevie hit the home button on her iPhone. The screen cut through the darkness like an electric torch.

"Ouch!" cried Tommy, raising his hands to protect his eyes. "You seared my pupils. Warn a guy before you do that."

"Sorry," laughed Eevie, "it got me too. You'd think I'd know better from our all night texting binges."

"I'll let you know what I think, as soon as I can see again. If anybody chases us, just shine that thing in their face; I could jog to Egypt before they'd be able to see again."

"So dramatic! OK, got it! We need to go to the main trail and then it's pretty much a direct path on the Widow Trail, with a few curves thrown in here and there."

"Great, they would have to name it Widow Trail," frowned Tommy.

"It's called Widow Trail because during the Revolutionary War, there was a horrible battle and many women lost their husbands here."

"Oh, that's really sad," said Tommy, picturing the battle in his mind. "I bet there are all kinds of artifacts buried here."

"Probably a…" Eevie's words hung in the air.

The skeletal branches seemed to reach so high that they became one with the inky sky above. The leaves, like tattered clothing, hung to the tips of the spiny branches—shimmering silver and black. In the shadowy darkness, the tree seemed to coil and uncoil, writhing as if…breathing.

"I guess we don't need your GPS app anymore," whispered Tommy.

Eevie didn't bother to reply. Her heart was pounding.

They took another step forward, their feet just on the edge of the vast network of roots spiraling outward from the tree.

"Why this tree? Why not a friendly looking tree like a juniper or a dogwood?"

"*Remember*, keep your feet off the roots," whispered Eevie forcefully. "Maybe this isn't such a great idea." Eevie's eyes were locked on the tree. Her chest rose and fell quickly as her breathing came in short bursts.

"I'm feeling the same way," whispered Tommy. "Let's just get some pictures and get out of here." Tommy shivered as he replayed the look the ranger gave him when he caught him in a lie.

Eevie nodded. She touched the ground with the tip of her sneaker and then tentatively took one more step toward the tree.

"Hurry, Eevie, just shoot some video. When the students see how creepy this tree is, they will believe anything we say!"

Eevie nodded. "OK, OK." The electronic ping sounded like a cannon, shattering the silence of the forest. The red record button glowed like the eye of a cyclops in the darkness. She slowly inched forward, pointing her phone at the top of the tree and then down the trunk, to the roots.

"There's not enough light—you can barely see it in the video."

"One second." Tommy kneeled down and found his flashlight. He played the light up and down the tree.

"Much better." Eevie slowly panned the camera up and down the tree.

Tommy cautiously inched forward. They were now less than fifteen feet from the tree as Eevie panned her phone upward through the branches.

"Eevie, that's enough. Come on, we don't need to push our luck!"

Eevie nodded. She knew he was right. Tommy knelt to put his flashlight back in his backpack. He paused—something wasn't right. Eevie's face grew taut. "Tommy, let's get out of here!" she screamed.

Eevie felt adrenaline rush through her like electricity. The ground was shaking and just as she began to run, Tommy's scream tore through her. She spun around. Tommy pitched forward, clawing at the roots that had wrapped around his leg. He beat at the root that had pinned him to the ground with the end of his flashlight. The light stabbed through the blackness like a laser with each downward blow. Eevie ran toward him, screaming. "Tommy!!!"

She grabbed his flailing arm and pulled with all her might. Tommy kicked out with his free foot and broke free. He scrambled backward to gain his footing.

"Run!" he screamed. "Run!!"

One step, two steps, and then he saw it. A thick root the size of a man's arm wrapped around Eevie's waist, mercilessly smashing her to the ground. She hit hard with a thud, knocking the wind out of her.

Eevie clawed at her waist. Ignoring the roots that encircled his feet, Tommy kicked free and ran over to Eevie, tearing at the enormous root that had coiled around her chest. Eevie panicked, thrashing her body and gasping for air. Tommy raised his arm and began chopping and pulling at the root wrapped around her. His eyes locked to hers, and her fear fed his rage. He ripped into the root until his fingers were bloody and torn.

"Let go of my FRIEND!!!" yelled Tommy, his voice enraged with desperate emotion.

Suddenly, the world seemed to drop from beneath them, and they fell into blackness.

DOES ANYONE HAVE AN ADVIL?

"Eevie!!! Eevie, WHERE ARE YOU?" Are you OK?!" gasped Tommy desperately. He moved his head from side to side trying to get his bearings.

"Yeah.... Yeah I think I'm OK!" answered Eevie, relieved just to feel air fill her lungs again.

"I dropped the flashlight. Sorry about that," said Tommy disappointedly. In the darkness, he rubbed his arms. The roots had torn right through his shirt, bruising and scraping his skin. He could feel the ragged remains of his fingernails as he rubbed his arms.

"It's OK—I've got my phone," Eevie said. Tommy turned his head as the light from Eevie's phone stabbed through the darkness.

Reflexively, he closed his eyes as bright dots now danced in front of him. "I promise I'll never say anything again about how bright your phone is," said Tommy, grateful to have some light in the inky blackness that surrounded them.

Tommy looked over at Eevie and saw that she was still lying on the ground.

"Eevie, can you stand?"

His question was met with silence. Illuminated in an orb of light, Tommy could see her holding her knee.

"Eevie," said Tommy more purposefully, "are you OK? Did you hurt your knee?" Tommy couldn't hide the worry that filled his voice.

"I don't know." Her face contorted in pain. "I fell right on it.... It really hurts."

"Can you try to stand?"

"Give me a minute, Tommy," she said, her voice wavering. He could hear the pain and frustration.

"Eevie, we should probably call for help. I don't know how badly you're hurt and..."

"Are you kidding?" said Eevie emphatically. "Our parents will kill us! Not to mention how much trouble we'll get in for trespassing in the park. We'll have to find a way out of here on our own." She hesitated. "Besides...my phone has no signal."

Tommy pressed the "home" button on his phone. The all too familiar "no signal" alert taunted him.

"Figures," muttered Tommy. "No signal here either."

Tommy's fingers swiped across his iPhone. Suddenly, his screen was filled with a fiery torch.

"What in God's earth is that?"

"It's a torch app. Instead of using the flashlight app, I downloaded this cool torch app. You have your GPS app; I have the 'mighty torch app.'"

"Tommy," said Eevie, shaking her head, "sometimes I truly worry about you."

The light from his iPhone flickered upward. The walls seemed smooth, yet vascular like skin. Just below the surface, Tommy could see thousands of roots that interconnected like neurons in a huge nervous system. Tommy reached out, his fingers trembling. The wall was cool beneath his fingertips and as hard as stone.

Eevie squeezed her eyes tightly as she attempted to straighten her leg. *I can do this. I have to do this.* Clenching her jaw, she gingerly straightened and bent her leg. *It does feel better to move it.*

"Eevie, are you sure you are going to be OK?"

Eevie could feel the worry in Tommy's voice.

"I'm going to get us out of here.... Somehow."

"I'll be fine—just give me a couple of minutes," Eevie smiled reassuringly, sounding more sure than she really was. "I think I just really bruised my knee. I've taken harder falls in soccer."

"OK, just don't push yourself."

Eevie began to answer, but instead just nodded and continued to massage her knee.

Holding his phone like a virtual torch, Tommy began slowly exploring the cave.

"This would be so much easier if there was an exit sign." Slowly, he turned like a human lighthouse, using the light to explore the vascular walls that surrounded them.

Tommy turned his torch light upward. Instinctually, he recoiled backward; the ceiling was a living, writhing twisted mass of roots.

"HOLY CRAP! 'UP' is OUT of the question. Not an option!"

"Are those snakes?" asked Eevie, shivering, her eyes wide with fear.

"No, those are roots, verrrry angry roots. When I get out of here, Ranger Rick or not, I'm going to bludgeon, insult, and then chainsaw the sap out of this tree."

Eevie turned and faced the wall on all fours. Using her hands against the wall, she slowly pushed herself up to a standing position. Her knee was still throbbing, but she could tell that nothing was broken.

Tommy watched her in silence, willing his friend to be OK.

She turned and slowly put her full weight onto her hurt leg. It was so painful it made her brain hurt. She took a tentative step. Then another, then another. Each step felt like she was kissing an electric eel, but the alternative—lying here in a dirt igloo for eternity—was not even an option.

"We are going to ignore the fact that I am temporarily limping. Understood?"

Tommy nodded, just happy to see his friend standing. "Got it. Please just take it easy. I'm just gonna try to find a way out of here before our phones run out of power."

"Maybe we should just use one at a time. I'll put mine on power saving mode," said Eevie.

"Good idea; I'm already suffering from Facebook withdrawal. Don't judge, it's a thing."

Eevie smiled; she knew Tommy was trying to make her feel better. "How wide do you think it is down here? Forty, fifty feet?"

"I don't know, Eevie. I'm just hoping there's a tunnel or something leading us out of here. There's no debris down here, so that gives me some hope that there is a way out."

A tiny electronic "bing" rang out from Tommy's phone.

Eevie inhaled excitedly. "Did you just get a message?"

Tommy shook his head. "Unfortunately, that's my phone's way of telling me that our relationship is about to end. It means my battery is at about fifteen percent."

"If we run out of light, we'll never find our way out of here."

"Then we better get moving." Tommy switched from the torch app to his flashlight. Eevie rubbed her hands across the surface of the huge chasm, searching for any hint of a way out. "I don't see anything but wall, and more wall. And in the darkness, how do we know that we haven't gone all the way around and we're just looking at the same thing?"

"Because we haven't reached my backpack yet," said Tommy. "I laid it up against the wall, so we'd know where we started."

Suddenly a flash of light caught Tommy's eyes. "What the..."

Tommy leaned in closer to the wall.

"What is it?" whispered Eevie, moving next to Tommy.

"A mirror, I think. I can't really tell—it's almost completely overgrown with roots.... Hold my phone; I'm gonna try and tear the roots away. These roots are all connected. Hopefully I'm not going to upset the root gods."

The roots looked like a massive spider web. Tommy looked at his hand, willing it to stop trembling. Curling his hand around a fistful of roots, he pulled. The roots ripped from the wall, raining dirt around Tommy and Eevie's feet. Both Eevie and Tommy stood motionless. Listening. Feeling. Getting ready to run. Eevie exhaled and then inhaled heavily; she hadn't realized that she had been holding her breath. Nothing...

Grabbing another handful of roots, Tommy tore them away from the wall, tossing them to the ground. He gasped as he watched them slither and burrow into the ground, becoming a part of the living ganglion of roots.

"OK, that's just creepy," shuddered Eevie.

"Eevie, it's a mirror," whispered Tommy excitedly. "And there is something written above it."

"What does it say?" Eevie's heart was racing.

"Objects in the rearview mirror may be closer than they appear."

Eevie closed her eyes and shook her head. "Seriously? Tommy, sometimes, I can't even find the words..."

"It says: 'The answer lies within you.' Clearly this tree was a philosophy major because I have no idea what that means."

A flash of hope appeared on Eevie's face. "Well, one thing's for sure, we are not the first ones down here. Someone had to put the mirror here, and write that message. So, there *has* to be a way out. We simply have to find it."

The mirror was long and narrow; the edges looked as if they had literally grown into the wall. Eevie looked more closely at the mirror, and her shadowy reflection stared back. Then she spotted something. She pulled more of the roots away. "There's a hole beneath the mirror."

"I probably made it when I pulled the roots out," said Tommy as he leaned in for a closer look.

"No. See, look, it's perfectly round."

"I don't know what it's for, Eevie. Maybe if we solve the puzzle we'll figure it out."

"'The answer lies within you' could mean anything. In your eyes, in your mind, in your heart. We could be here for days trying to figure out what 'lies within us.'"

"And why would they put a mirror here...unless it was something you could see...or maybe figure out by looking at ourselves."

"Maybe it's a two-way mirror and we're being watched right now," Eevie said.

"OK, that is beyond creepy."

Tommy stood and stared into the mirror; he stared into his own eyes. "The answer lies within," he whispered. He moved his face closer to the mirror. "What lies within?"

"Tommy, do that again." Eevie moved beside him, staring at the mirror.

"Do what?"

"Never mind—move out of the way!"

Tommy took a step back. Eevie moved her face until it was less than half an inch from the mirror. She opened her mouth, breathed out, and made a "haaaaaaaa" sound. Her breath immediately fogged the mirror, and in the midst of the fog, she could see three letters. "T-E-R."

"Do it again, Eevie! Do it again! Something is written on the mirror," said Tommy excitedly.

"I know, I know!"

Eevie leaned in again, this time moving her face slowly across the width of the mirror as she exhaled. Like magic, the letters began to appear.

"W-A-T-E-R."

"Water? The answer is 'water'?" asked Tommy, confused. "How is that supposed to help us?"

"I don't know. Maybe there are more words and I missed them."

"I'll try..."

Eevie's and Tommy's eyes grew wide. The word "water" was melting, creating a silver liquid stream, like wax from a candle—pooling toward the bottom of the mirror. A silver drop of liquid fell like a tear from the mirror to the ground.

"Maybe," said Tommy, leaning in closer to the hole, "we're supposed to put that liquid in the hole beneath the mirror! It said water, so maybe we put the water in the hole."

Another drop fell to the ground.

"I don't know, Tommy," said Eevie worriedly, shaking her head.

"Well, if we don't try something, it's all going to just drip down from the mirror. I'm going to at least try. I'll catch a drop on my finger and put it in the hole. It will either work or not."

Tommy quickly extended his index finger before he could change his mind. He watched as the silvery droplet paused momentarily at the bottom of the mirror and then dropped to his fingertip. It felt like ice, then like fire. Tommy closed his eyes in pain and put his finger in the hole.

"AHHHHHH!" screamed Tommy.

Eevie watched in horror as the hole closed on Tommy's finger. Tommy's pain was unbearable. "Eevie, my hand!" Another silvery drop fell onto the back of Tommy's hand, searing his flesh, which immediately blistered.

I Really Should Have Paid Attention in Latin Class

Tommy screamed out in pain. He gritted his teeth and pulled. Hot tears streamed down his cheeks. *If I pull any harder, I'm going to rip my finger off my hand!* Eevie frantically scratched and clawed at the wall.

"Turn your hand, Tommy! Turn your hand before it drips on you again!"

Pain surged through Tommy's body. He felt his lips going numb, and he fought the dizzying blackness that was beginning to creep over him, itching his scalp. Eevie caught him as his knees buckled.

"Breathe, Tommy! Breathe! I'll dig you out!"

Tears of pain escaped from Tommy's closed eyes as he fought off wave after wave of dizziness.

The silvery drops fell to the ground more quickly, and Eevie noticed that it had devoured the dirt and roots, burning right through them. She saw a glint of metal.

"Tommy! I think I see a key! I think it's a key!" she screamed excitedly.

Eevie clawed frantically at the dirt. "It's a ring, Tommy," said Eevie, her voice filling with fear. "I think this is what we were supposed to put in the hole."

Tears poured down Eevie's cheeks. "I'm so sorry, Tommy."

"Eevie, it's not your fault." Tommy gritted his teeth. "I'm the idiot who put my finger in the hole. It's numb now, Eevie. I can't feel it anymore...." Tommy looked at his friend. "None of this is your fault. We'll get out of here."

Eevie looked at the ring. It was an intricately crafted, coiled snake. Its red fangs glistened like diamonds, piercing its own tail to complete the circle. The underside of the ring was polished smooth with the word "Retexo" etched into its belly.

"Tommy, the ring says 'Retexo.' What does that mean?"

Tommy shook his head in frustration. "I have no idea, but I do know who does. I have a translator app on my phone. There's an app called World Translate. Open that and type in 'Retexo,' and hurry!"

"Oh yeah! I've got the same app." Eevie's fingers danced across the screen. As the app opened, the battery dropped to 3 percent. The flashlight app had burned through the last remaining bit of his battery. *Come on. Come on,* screamed Eevie in her head.

"Untwist!" screamed Eevie. "It's Latin for untwist!"

Eevie squatted, placing the phone on her knee. Holding the ring between her index fingers and thumbs, she began twisting the ring in every direction. Suddenly, the ring unhinged and opened.

"Tommy, I'm going to put this ring over your finger. I can't promise you, but EVERYTHING inside of me is telling me that this is what we were supposed to put in the hole."

"It's fine, Eevie." Tommy smiled a sad smile. "At this point I don't think my finger's gonna mind."

Eevie gently put the ring around the base of Tommy's finger. One last drip of silvery water fell from the mirror, hitting the ring. Their eyes widened as a serpent came to life, slithering around Tommy's finger. The serpent rotated fully around his finger and then without warning sank its red fangs into it. Tommy collapsed to his knees in pain, his finger still stuck in the wall.

Eevie screamed and tried to pry the snake from Tommy's finger. The harder she pulled, the tighter the snake coiled around it.

"Stop, Eevie, just stop!" yelled Tommy angrily. "Just stop!"

Eevie pulled back, shocked. "I was just trying to help."

"I'm sorry, Eevie. I'm sorry."

They watched as the snake's head rose to look at Tommy and then Eevie. A drop of crimson clung to the bottom of the snake's fang. The snake then coiled tightly around Tommy's finger and dug its fangs into its own tail. They watched in disbelief as the snake turned back into metal.

The hole suddenly released Tommy's finger. He fell backward, holding his hand. Waves of agonizing pain pulsed through his finger over and over as the blood and feeling returned. Eevie crouched beside her friend, grasping his shoulder. He was free, but at what price? In the darkness, Tommy gently tugged at the ring. Pain seared through his finger, causing him to inhale sharply. *I guess I won't be taking that off any time soon*, Tommy told himself.

Eevie looked up; she could feel air on her face. Where was it coming from? She flipped Tommy's phone over and touched the screen. It was dead. *Of course.* Staring into the darkness, she could just make out a faint, shimmering light.

"Tommy, can you see that? Can you feel that air? I feel air."

Tommy pushed himself to his feet. "I see it, Eevie! If there's fresh air, then that's got to be our way out!"

A thick ribbon of light framed the outside of the mirror. Eevie reached forward and gently touched the surface of the mirror. Suddenly, thousands of jagged lines appeared across the surface. They both watched in stunned silence as the mirror collapsed in a shiny, silvery cloud of dust. Light burst through the cavern, blinding them. Instinctively, they turned away from the bright light.

"Second time. Second time my eyes have been seared," groaned Tommy, his hand covering his eyes.

Slowly, Eevie opened her fingers a little to let some of the light in. She slowly turned in a circle, seeing for the first time the inside of the cavern. The walls and the ceiling were made of dirt and rock, and a living, vascular bundle comprised of thousands of roots intertwined. *What made this place? Who made this place?*

Tommy walked over and grabbed his backpack. He looked up at the gnarled and twisted ceiling. The roots had shifted and moved; no one would ever know that two children had been ensnared and mercilessly thrown into oblivion.

Tommy shook his head in the affirmative. The voice inside his head said, *You figured out the mirror; you've got this*. Another voice in his head answered resolutely. *Yes, I do*.

Eevie leaned forward, looking down through the opening.

"Tommy, it looks like a lake—with glowing rocks."

"A lake with glowing rocks? There's a lake at the park, so maybe it's the underground part of that lake."

"I hope so." Eevie continued staring. "How long do you think we've been down here?"

Tommy knew where this was going. "About an hour, Eevie. We still have a chance to get out of here before our parents start worrying. Right now, we need to focus on getting out of here in one piece." Tommy glanced down at his hand. He was glad to still have his finger—even though now it was permanently adorned with an evil serpent.

Without another word, Eevie slowly climbed through the opening. She paused, sitting on the ledge, then pulled her phone from her pocket. "Tommy, my phone, it's not waterproof."

"It's fine. My backpack is waterproof; I'll put your phone in there. How deep does it look?"

"It's pretty deep, Tommy, ten feet or more."

"I have a suggestion to make, and it's not because I want to see your pasty white legs, so get that thought out of your head. But we probably shouldn't try to swim in sweatpants, sneakers, and hoodies."

Eevie contemplated what Tommy was saying for a moment. He was right; her wet clothes would drag her down and exhaust her. She climbed back through the opening. Tommy was digging through his backpack looking for clothes for Eevie.

"Eevie, I have my gym shorts and a T-shirt. You can put those on."

"Thank you, Tommy," smiled Eevie. "You truly are one of the last remaining gentlemen."

"Careful, Eeves, so many compliments—my head may not fit through our magical window over there."

Tommy turned his head while Eevie got dressed, then he quickly removed everything except for his boxers and a T-shirt.

"I'm going to put our clothes in the backpack," yelled Tommy.

"I think we'll be fine," Eevie called out. "It's pretty warm down here."

"As long as the water isn't freezing, I'll be fine. I hate cold water."

Tommy smiled. Eevie was wearing his team's workout clothes. She had tied a knot in the band of his elastic shorts. A knot also adorned the bottom of his T-shirt, pulling it snug against her.

"Go, Titans!" laughed Tommy.

Eevie shook her head. "I take back everything I said about you being a gentleman."

"What? I'm simply full of team spirit."

"You're full of something, and it's not 'team spirit,'" said Eevie, making air quotes with her fingers.

Like déjà vu, Eevie climbed through the narrow opening that had once been the mirror. Tommy stood right behind her. Pushing off the edge, she dropped with a splash into the water. Inside, Tommy was beyond worried that his best friend was jumping into a lake of acid water. He was waiting for the screams and had secretly tied their hoodies together in a makeshift rope in case he needed to quickly pull her out of the water.

Eevie kicked her legs twice and broke the surface of the water. It was cool, but not uncomfortable.

She looked up at Tommy's worried face and immediately smiled. "All's good—come on down."

Tommy let out an audible sigh of relief. "OK. Watch out below!" He threw the backpack on his back, climbed through the opening, and with a "GERONIMO," he jumped into the water.

Eevie and Tommy grasped an outcrop of rock. Before them, a vast expanse of water glistened for what seemed a hundred feet or more. This cavern was different. Jagged rock formations, like small cities, erupted from the floor and walls of the cavern. The water was illuminated by huge luminescent rocks, giving the water a silvery blue color.

Though there was no wind to speak of, the water seemed to be moved by an invisible current. The only noise was the gentle sound of water splashing up on the rocks.

The bottom of the lake was covered in a muddy sand, with green fernlike vegetation swaying in the gentle undercurrent.

"Eevie," said Tommy, pointing at a spot directly across the lake from them. "There's a large ledge on the other side, where we can look around. Do you think you can swim across?"

"Yeah, I think so. I'm not the best swimmer in the world, but it looks like it's about the same width of our football field."

"If you look in the center..." Tommy pointed to the middle of the water. "...there's a bunch of tall rocks or something. We can swim there, rest for a minute, and then swim the rest of the way."

Eevie's eyes followed Tommy's outstretched finger. "Yeah, I see them. Let's do it."

They slowly swam toward the ledge. They were halfway across the lake when Tommy stopped and began treading water. Directly in front of them stood an army of rocky columns. Tommy descended below the surface for a better look. Dozens of columns stood before him. Each column connected to the other by what could only be described as a network of interconnected roots that had dug themselves into the silty bottom of the lake.

"Eevie," said Tommy wiping the water from his eyes. "They're like giant trees with huge roots, like they grew here. Some of them are wider and taller than the others, like a forest full of trees."

Eevie nodded. "A forest full of trees with letters and numbers on them."

"They look so smooth and..." Tommy reached out to touch a column, but as soon as his finger made contact, it crumbled into pieces, releasing a black, swirling mist that swarmed and turned and twisted in the air like a million angry mosquitos. Reflexively, Tommy and Eevie slammed their palms to their ears—the black swarm made a screeching sound so loud they thought their eardrums would explode.

The black cloud swirled above their heads and then crashed into the water. The water began bubbling and churning. Suddenly the water became much hotter. The black liquid rose above them, forming into five words: "What Erodes and Then Revives." There was an ear-piercing scream as the words shattered into nothingness.

Tommy could barely breathe. His heart pounded in his throat and his ears rang from the screeching. He began repeating the phrase "What Erodes and Then Revives" over and over in his head, frightened he'd forget it.

He could see Eevie's mouth moving but her words sounded garbled like a broken speaker. She was jabbing her finger in the air, pointing across the lake.

Tommy turned his head. It took just a moment, and then he saw them. The top half of four humongous recessed wooden doors peeked above the water's surface. One could have easily missed seeing them because they were directly under a huge, rocky over-hang casting a deep shadow over the partially submerged doors. Suddenly, a metallic groaning sound cut through the air. Tommy shook his head. *Did one of the doors just slide upward a little?*

Eevie's eyes widened. She reached out and grasped Tommy's shoulder, making him jump.

"Don't do that!" he exclaimed.

Eevie ignored his outburst. "Tommy, did that door just move?" she whispered.

"I'm not sure; I'll check it out. Keep treading water and don't touch ANYTHING!"

Eevie nodded. "What are you going to...?" Tommy's head disappeared below the silvery surface into a sea of bubbles. It took only a moment for Tommy's eyes to adjust. Four large wooden gates jutted upward from the silty bottom, cutting upward through the water at least another ten feet.

Whoa, those things are massive!

Mounted beside each gate was a lantern, each burning a different colored flame—white, gold, red, and yellow.

Tommy exhaled hard, releasing a stream of bubbles. "What the...!"

TOMMY, OR SHOULD I SAY EINSTEIN...

The giant door with the red lantern had risen about a foot. Beneath the door, bathed in red light, two giant, hairy insect legs scraped and clawed furiously at the ground trying to get out.

Tommy exploded upward from the water. "Eevie, get to the other side! Don't touch anything—get to the other side!"

"What is it?!" she screamed at Tommy.

"All I could see were the legs! They looked like massive spider legs! Go!"

All thoughts about whether or not they could swim across the lake disappeared. In a matter of seconds, they dragged themselves out of the water onto the large rock ledge. Struggling to catch their breath, they sat staring toward the gates.

"Tommy, if it's a huge spider...," panted Eevie. "It's another puzzle, isn't it?"

Eevie put her hands to her face and closed her eyes. She simply wanted to cry, for all of this to be over—but she knew she couldn't have a defeatist attitude and make it through this nightmare. She looked over at Tommy. He was wading in the shallow water, his head down, looking for something. Her head moved as if she were watching a tennis match. Check the gates to see if they moved again; make sure Tommy is OK. Check the gates; make sure Tommy is OK. She relaxed when she saw that he had found what he was looking for, and he returned safely to the rock's ledge.

Tommy quickly dropped to his hands and knees and, using a piece of what appeared to be limestone, etched "What Erodes and Then Revives" onto the ledge.

Tommy rocked back onto his heels and relieved himself of his backpack. "C'mon Eevie," he said, calling her over. "This puzzle's not gonna solve itself, and I have yet another amazing plan."

"What's your brilliant plan?" asked Eevie, sitting beside him, her spirit lifting.

"There are about thirty poles out there. Each one has a letter and a number, and my guess is...that they mean something."

Eevie nodded her head, looking impressed. "OK, keep going, Einstein."

"That's all I got."

Eevie closed her eyes and groaned. "We're gonna die."

"So dramatic," said Tommy, gazing out over the water stoically.

Eevie arched her eyebrows. "You know, if I wasn't so afraid of dying alone, I'd beat you to a pulp."

"I guess I'm pretty safe then, unless you plan on befriending the lovely spider over there. I'm sure it would *love* some company."

Eevie shuddered at the thought. "OK, we need to focus. Let's type what we know so far and see if we can figure out what we need to do next."

Tommy looked down where he had scrawled the black swarm's message. He looked up at Eevie.

"Eevie, let's save your battery and just write on the rock."

"Good idea. You're edging back to your Einstein title."

"OK." Eevie closed her eyes. Tommy flashed back to school in his mind's eye. He could see Eevie safe and sound sitting in class, her eyes closed, deep and thought. How quickly things had changed.

Eevie opened her eyes. "Here's what we know. There are about thirty poles with letters and numbers. There are four stone doors, each with a different colored lantern—red, yellow, white, and gold."

"Hang on one second. It's not easy transferring dictation to stone." Tommy's fingers were already beginning to cramp as he struggled with his rudimentary writing implement.

Tommy looked up. "We can't forget our last clue: 'WATER.' We also know that red door number four is not a happy place."

Eevie looked around. "Right now, the only way I see out of here is those four doors, and we have no idea what's behind the other three."

"OK. Well, I guess you work on the puzzle, and I'll start swimming for clues."

"Good lu..." Eevie's voice trailed off and she squinted and leaned forward. "Tommy, I think I saw a shadow in the water."

Tommy looked out over the water. "As long as those doors stay down, I think we'll be fine. We just can't make any more mistakes. However," said Tommy smiling at Eevie, "thanks to you, I have a serious case of the heebie-jeebies, so before I begin my aquatic quest, I'm going to make sure Mr. Spider is still behind his door."

Tommy slowly slid off the rock ledge into the water. He held his breath as the warm water flowed around him. He blinked a couple of times and his eyes cleared. He could see the huge hairy legs stretched out underneath the door. Whatever it was—spider, mutant grasshopper—it was still trapped. Tommy rose to the surface and breathed a sigh of relief. "Your new best friend is still behind the door—all's good."

"OK. Please be careful, and don't touch anything!"

Tommy gave Eevie a thumbs-up and began his trek around the lake. Below the surface, the floor of the lake was soft and silty with clumps of reeds and green leafy vegetation. What did grow looked like long, wispy blades of grass that gently swayed with the water's current. Huge stones lay scattered, giving off a weird iridescent glow. The walls were gray and rocky, just like one would expect in an underwater cavern.

Tommy carefully examined the craggy walls as he swam the perimeter of the lake. *I hope that Eevie's having better luck than me, because there is nothing down here but rock, and more rock.*

Tommy broke the surface and gave Eevie a thumbs-up. "Nothing yet!" he called out.

Eevie was crouched down on her knees, her hand busily carving into the rock. She waved an OK, then turned back to writing.

Tommy lowered beneath the surface and began patiently examining the rocky walls again. There was nothing but rocks, and more rocks. Tommy was beginning his ascent when he noticed a huge shadow over him. Immediately, he clutched onto the wall, pulling himself as far as he could underneath an outcrop of rock. *What the heck is that?*

Tommy's eyes bulged as the shadow passed over him. He stared, not daring to move as the huge creature swam slowly above him. After it passed over Tommy, he cautiously and quietly rose to the surface. His simple task of "finding a way out" had just become a little more complicated.

I better warn Eevie before she tries to go into the water. Tommy watched as the creature slowly moved farther and farther away. He slowly rose to the surface and quietly sucked in a huge gulp of much needed air.

Eevie squinted as she stared out at the columns of stone. She could make out a few numbers and letters, but to see the rest she would need to have a closer vantage point. So far she had scraped A-12, B-7, C-25, D-16, and E-21 onto the rock.

She looked out over the water to find Tommy. She slowly scanned the surface and the walls, but he was nowhere to be seen. *I'll just swim out to the columns and begin memorizing a few at a time.*

Eevie slowly slid into the water and began swimming toward the rock columns.

Tommy was almost halfway across the lake when he spotted Eevie swimming toward the columns. His heart jumped. He wanted to yell, but he was afraid that the beast would attack them. Eevie swam into the forest of stone columns, staring upward. G3, H6. She turned her head downward just in time to see Tommy quickly swimming toward her.

"Eevie! Eevie!" he urgently whispered.

Tommy's mind exploded into stars as he was struck from below. His flailing body flew through the air, crashing into several columns. Instantly they collapsed into the water, releasing multiple screeching black swarms into the air. Their shrill cries were deafening. Tommy's limp body began to sink, bubbles rushing to the surface as his lungs filled with water.

"No!!!" screamed Eevie.

Eevie swam as fast as she could to Tommy. Diving downward she could see his lifeless body lying on the floor of the lake. Above her, the shrill black cloud screeched and then plunged into the water, throwing up a wall of silt and bubbles. Instantly the temperature of the water rose twenty degrees or more. A bellowing cry shook the cavern as the behemoth that had struck Tommy arched through the air, screaming in pain. Eevie's mouth gaped open. It looked like a giant whale with enormous curled tusks on either side of its head. It crashed into the lake, creating a splash that sent burning hot water to the ceiling of the cave. Scalding hot waves burned Eevie's face and eyes. She struggled to get her bearings as the giant beast launched out of the water again—crying out in agony.

Another onslaught of waves buffeted Eevie. She was by no means a strong swimmer, but she had raw adrenaline coursing through her veins. She dove downward with all her strength. Below the surface, the water had become a whirlwind of debris. With her hands outstretched, she swam toward the bottom. Finally, her hands felt Tommy's chest.

She reached her arms around Tommy's torso and tried to swim upward. Eevie began to panic; she had seen lifeguards grab the person from behind and swim, but was she strong enough to swim with one arm supporting Tommy? She'd have to try!

Quickly she swam behind him. Reaching her arm under his arm, she cradled his head on her shoulder. *Here we go, Tommy, hang on.* Eevie's lungs were burning as she forcefully kicked off from the bottom. Her head broke through the surface, and Tommy's head lolled from side to side on her shoulder. Eevie fought to stay afloat. Time after time she went under, gulping water into her lungs, choking as she fought to make it to land.

Slipping and sliding, she dragged Tommy up onto the rocky ledge. Pulling her wet hair from her face, she placed her ear to his mouth. Nothing. She placed her fingers to her friend's neck to feel for a pulse. *Nothing.* She quickly leaned his head back and pinched his nose. She blew into his mouth, filling his lungs. She watched as his chest rose and fell. She blew into his mouth again. *Nothing.* She moved to Tommy's side, tears streaming down her face.

"Tommy, please!" she screamed. Placing her hands on his chest, she began rapid compressions. "One Mississippi, two Mississippi..."

After thirty chest compressions, she quickly gave him two more breaths.

Tommy's lips had lost all their color, and Eevie screamed his name. "Tommy!" She shook his shoulders in desperation.

Her hands clasped over one another again: "One Mississippi, two Mississippi, thr..."

It Had to Be a Spider...

Tommy's head flew back, and he began to vomit water and the contents of his stomach. Eevie quickly rolled him onto his side, cradling his head on her knees. Tommy began coughing and retching.

"It's OK, Tommy. It's OK," Eevie whispered. For what seemed like an eternity, Tommy lay still, not moving. His breath was ragged and shallow.

"Thank you, Eevie," whispered Tommy hoarsely.

Eevie simply nodded, her body convulsing, the raw emotion hitting her in waves. She had saved her best friend's life...she had saved her best friend's life. Hot tears ran down her cheeks, falling into his hair.

Tommy tried to sit up as waves of nausea and dizziness coursed through his body.

"Rest, Tommy, just rest."

Tommy smiled a weak smile up at Eevie, his voice caught in his throat as he saw the tears coursing down his friend's face.

"I'm OK, Eevie.... You rock. What the heck was that thing? It looked like a whale."

"I think you're right," nodded Eevie. "It looked like a whale with tusks...long, curvy tusks like an elephant's."

"At least I didn't get impaled. I just happened to have the misfortune of being over it when it decided to breach. I don't think it meant to harm me. It could have skewered me and had me for dinner if it wanted."

Eevie smiled. The color had returned to Tommy's lips and he was able to sit up.

"Tommy, I need to get the rest of the clues. Will you be OK for a few minutes? I promise I'll keep a close eye on our friends."

Tommy's eyes suddenly flew open wide. "Eevie, I crashed into more columns. Is our spider friend still in his cave?"

"I...I have no idea. I was so worried about getting you to shore that I forgot about everything else."

Tommy looked intently at Eevie. "Please tell me that spiders can't swim. Out of all the creatures in the world, even the hairless newt, I hate spiders." Tommy shivered as he thought about it.

They both turned their heads in the direction of the caves.

"Well," said Eevie in a soft but determined voice, "there's no way to tell without going in the water."

Tommy opened his mouth to argue, but he knew she was right. The only way to solve the puzzle was to get the numbers and letters off the columns. Hopefully he hadn't destroyed the ones that they needed.

Without another word, Eevie slowly slid underwater, keeping her back pressed against the rock ledge in case she had to quickly pull herself back up to safety. The water was painfully hot.

Eevie let her eyes adjust and then took in her surroundings. A surge of panic shot through her. The spider's gate was now fully open and another gate had raised about a foot. She could see a huge clawed foot, like a lizard's foot, clawing at the opening.

About thirty feet away she could see the enormous whale creature using its tusks to move large rocks, and eating whatever it was that lay underneath. *Maybe Tommy was right. The whale looks like an herbivore, probably harmless.*

Keeping her position against the ledge, she scanned the entire lake as well as she could. *No sign of Mr. Spider. Not good; he could be anywhere.*

Eevie pulled herself up out of the water. Tommy had grabbed the backpack and was eating a candy bar.

He looked at Eevie expectantly. "Anything? Did you see the spider?"

"The spider's gate is open, but I didn't see the spider, so I'm not sure where it is."

Tommy shook his head, his mind already going to horrible places. "Great, it had to be a spider."

"We've got the clues up to the letter G. I'm going to swim out and start calling them out to you. It's our only chance to get out of here."

"Let's do it."

Eevie slid into the water and opened her eyes. In the distance, she could still see the whale flipping up stones and tearing at leafy underwater vegetation. She quickly scanned the perimeter of the lake. *No spider.*

Eevie reached the stone forest and began to call out to Tommy— "H-6, I-10, K-22, L-18."

Some of the columns had been destroyed when Tommy was flung into them. The J, the P, and several other letters were missing.

"Slow down!" shouted Tommy, furiously trying to scrape the clues onto the rock. "I want to make sure it's legible."

"OK!" shouted Eevie, looking nervously around. *I just want to get out of this water.*

Several minutes later, Eevie was on her way back to the ledge. Tommy had scrawled out all of the clues into rows.

A-12, B-7, C-25, D-16, E-21, F-4, G-3,

H-6, I-10, K-22, L-18, M-24, N-5, O-15,

Q-23, R-19, S-20, T-2, W-1, Y-8, Z-14

"Don't mock my artistic integrity—it's not easy writing with a rock."

Eevie smiled. The jagged chalky letters and numbers looked like a small child had written out the clues. "It's legible," smiled Eevie. "That's all I care about."

"I have an idea," said Tommy. "The last clue was water; we could start there." Tommy etched out: W-1, A-12, T-2, E-21, R-19. "So it comes out to WATER and 1, 12, 2, 21, 19. We could start there," suggested Tommy.

"Do we really want to risk touching the wrong columns?" asked Eevie, studying the clues. "Bad things happen when we make mistakes, and if we make that water any hotter, we won't survive in it for more than a minute."

"Well, there are infinite combinations of letters and numbers, and we either try something or we sit here and do nothing."

Tommy grabbed the rock that they were using as a makeshift pencil. He stood wobbly and hurled the rock into the stone columns.

It struck one of the columns and it exploded into pieces. They covered their ears as the black swarm swirled skyward. The whale creature shrieked in pain, hurling itself out of the water.

"Tommy, stop! Stop!" screamed Eevie. "We're killing that creature." Tommy watched as the creature bellowed, throwing itself into the air and crashing down into the water. It began swimming toward the ledge.

It's coming right at us!

The whale struck the ledge, and huge stalactites came crashing down around them. Eevie screamed, falling backwards.

Tommy stood frozen, staring into the whale's eyes. The whale moaned, clearly in pain. Tommy wasn't sure why, but he slowly walked over to the whale. He had never been this close to such a majestic creature.

"We're sorry," he sobbed. "We didn't mean to hurt you. We're trapped in here and we're just trying to get out."

Gently he reached out and touched the whale's skin. It felt rubbery and slick, but incredibly hot.

The whale made a vibrating sound, deep in its throat.

"We'll figure this out," said Tommy quietly. "We have to."

Eevie stood beside Tommy, looking at the huge, beautiful creature. The whale moved itself half on the ledge, half off.

"It's cooler out of the water," said Tommy, "but it's gonna have to go back in soon." Eevie gently touched the whale and turned to Tommy. "We gotta figure this puzzle out without making any more mistakes."

"Eevie, if we stay with the idea that the clue is WATER, then what do the numbers stand for?"

Eevie walked back to the clues. She read "1, 12, 2, 21, 19" out loud. "If I add them together, I get 55. That doesn't make any sense."

"Eevie!" yelled Tommy. "What about the alphabet? They could be letters."

Eevie looked at Tommy. "You may have regained your genius status."

She quickly grabbed a rock. "1 would be A, 12 would be...," she began to recite the alphabet in her head. "L. 2 would be B. 21 would be..." She began reciting the alphabet again. "U. and 19 would be S.... ALBUS?"

"Like ALBUS Dumbledore? If he's behind one of those doors, we could really use him right now."

For the thousandth time in her life, Eevie looked at him and shook her head.

"Maybe it's a word scramble." She began scrawling out letters on the rock, but nothing made sense.

"Tommy." Eevie looked up with a smile on her face. "I think *Albus* is Latin, like the word *Retexo* on your ring."

Tommy glanced down at his swollen finger and the serpent that had made his finger its home.

Eevie ran over to the backpack and pulled out her phone. Her fingers flew across the screen as she fired up the World Translate app.

Excitedly, she typed A-L-B-U-S. She nearly dropped her phone with excitement. "Tommy! *Albus* is Latin for white! The color white! The door that we need is the 'white' door."

"Awesome," smiled Tommy. "We just need to touch the A-L-B-U-S columns." Tommy knelt down and touched the water. It was at the point of boiling.

"Eevie, we wouldn't last but a few seconds in this water. How are we supposed to get to the columns and get to the 'white' door?"

They both whipped their heads around as the giant whale lowered itself into the water. It swam to the columns and then returned back to the ledge. Steam rose from its body as it struggled to move onto the rocky ledge out of the water.

"Tommy, I think the whale may know something we don't know. It just swam a circle around the columns."

The immense creature was staring at them. It slipped back into the water and swam until it was alongside the ledge where they stood. Still staring, it smacked its tail on the water's surface.

Eevie turned and smiled at Tommy. "I know what it wants."

Eevie turned and walked toward the whale. Tommy raised his hand to protest. "Ee...!" She cut him short.

"I'll be fine," she said reassuringly.

Eevie climbed onto the giant beast, slipping and sliding on its wet, rubbery skin. *Tommy was right,* said Eevie to herself as her feet splashed into the water. *A few seconds in this water, and I'd be done.*

"Whale done," said Tommy, trying to let Eevie know she was OK, even though his best friend had just climbed on top of a huge aquatic beast that had unintentionally nearly killed him.

Eevie turned and waved to Tommy as the whale carried her toward the columns, and hopefully freedom.

Tommy stumbled backwards over a huge stalactite that had fallen from the cavern's ceiling. He landed hard on his hands and butt. He shook his head, clearing away the stars that danced across his vision. Then he stopped shaking his head and sat very still. The cave reminded him of a huge mouth, and as his eyes traversed the ceiling of the cave, he realized that the thousands of jagged stalagmites that patiently grew downward toward the surface of the lake looked like shark teeth.

Did one of those rocks just move?

Eevie and Tommy Grow Gills – Well kind-of...

Tommy slowly crab-walked further up the ledge, staring at the ceiling. *Whoosh.* Tommy could hear Eevie pushing the columns; it was working. No more explosions; no more skin-crawling, screeching things shooting into the air.

There it was again; the rock had moved. Tommy stared at the ceiling, and his body began to shake. The harder he tried to control his body, the more his body betrayed him. The all too familiar pounding of his heart in his ears.... Now Tommy could see it—eight black, saucer-sized orbs staring at him. He was being hunted, and on this ledge, there was no escape.

Tommy's fear became a reality. The massive spider slowly lowered itself from the ceiling onto the rocky ledge, never taking its eyes off Tommy, its prey.

Somewhere in the back of his mind he heard Eevie scream. The spider stood as tall as a horse, and its shiny black body gleamed. Its razor-sharp fangs were the size of Tommy's arms. Tommy screamed as it crawled toward him, and he crawled backwards as fast as he could, his eyes locked onto the spider's eyes. Venom dripped from the spider's fangs in anticipation of a delicious human meal.

Tommy watched in horror as the spider reared back and drove his head downward to impale Tommy with its fangs. Tommy balled up his body, throwing his arms over his head. He clenched his teeth and closed his eyes. His body shook with a sudden impact. The whale had crashed into the ledge where he lay, just as the spider was striking, causing the spider's fangs to smash into the stone inches away from Tommy's legs.

Tommy's eyes flew open—he was still alive! In front of him, the giant spider let out a shriek as it whipped its head back and forth to pull its fangs free of the stone.

"Tommy!" screamed Eevie. "Run!"

Tommy scrambled backwards trying to get his feet under him. The spider twisted and pulled, using its entire body. One fang broke free, showering Tommy with rock. The spider twisted his body, blocking Tommy's escape. It shrieked again and tore its head backwards, breaking the other fang free.

Tommy ran backwards, tripping over a rock. He fell hard onto his shoulder, pain rocketing through his body, his temples pounding so hard he thought they just might explode.

The spider stopped advancing for a moment and spun around. Eevie was hurling rocks at the spider.

"Eevie! No!" screamed Tommy.

The spider let out a blood-curdling screech and ran toward her. The spider's speed was incredible, and Eevie barely escaped into the water beside the whale.

In that instant, Tommy saw a chance. Beside him lay a four-foot, razor-sharp stalactite that had broken loose from the ceiling. With the spider distracted, Tommy quickly stood, and struggling mightily, he raised the stalactite with the point facing upward like a spear. He stepped in front of it, hiding it with his body. The spider spun around, its eight black eyes locked in on its prey. Tommy's body was trembling; he felt like vomiting. Eevie, not able to see the stalactite behind Tommy, was screaming for him to run.

The spider leapt into the air. The blackness covered Tommy. He felt the weight of the spider coming down on him. Quickly he dropped beside the stone spear, as he fought to hold it upright with all his might. The spider screeched as the rock spear ripped through its abdomen and back. Tommy snaked backwards and black inky liquid gushed onto him. The spider, writhing in pain, crawled toward Tommy, its fangs crashing into the rock in front of him. Tommy quickly climbed over a boulder and dove into the water. The spider half crawled and half dragged itself after him, and with an incredible scream it dove into the water on top of Tommy. Tommy tried to go deeper as the spider's spiky legs fought to wrap around him. Suddenly, there was a powerful rush of bubbles above him as the whale, using its tusks, impaled the spider and then used its head like a battering ram, crushing the spider to bits on the side of the ledge. The water turned an oily black as the carcass of the spider slowly sank to the bottom of the lake.

Tommy kicked up to the surface, sputtering and shaking his head. Eevie swam toward him and threw her arms around him.

"OK. OK," sputtered Tommy, "you're gonna make Fred jealous."

"Who?" said Eevie, a look of confusion filling her face.

"The whale," laughed Tommy.

"You named the whale Fred?" gasped Eevie, looking mortified. "That's the best you could do? This beautiful, epic, immense creature, and you choose Fred? What if it's a girl?" said Eevie as the whale swam up beside them.

Tommy could see both his and Eevie's images reflected in the whale's beautiful, gold-speckled eye. He reached out gently, touching the whale's head.

"If it's a girl," said Tommy, smiling, "I'll name her Fredericka."

Eevie rubbed the whale's head. "We're sorry to have caused you so much pain. You saved our lives—thank you."

The whale's tremendous body vibrated, like a cat purring. The water had cooled, the spider was dead, the white door was open, revealing a massive tunnel, and hopefully it would lead them to freedom.

Tommy and Eevie swam back over to the ledge. Tommy grabbed his backpack and Eevie sat on the ledge, her feet dangling in the water.

Eevie was exhausted, emotionally and physically. But she had surprised herself. Unimaginable things had happened to her and she had stood up to the challenges; in moments of danger where she could have been killed, she chose friendship over her own safety. And because of her bravery, her best friend was now coming over to sit beside her. She smiled to herself. *I can't imagine anything better than a true best friend.*

Tommy sat beside her and opened the backpack. He dug down through their clothes to the bottom of the bag, retrieving a couple of power bars and a Gatorade.

Eevie's eyes grew wide when she saw the power bar. She quickly grabbed one and devoured it in three bites.

Tommy took a swig and handed it to Eevie. "I'm glad I got my fingers off that thing."

"Are there any more?" asked Eevie.

"There are two more power bars and one more Gatorade."

Tommy handed her the Gatorade. She quickly drank most of the bottle without stopping to take a breath. She was so thirsty she simply couldn't stop herself.

"I'm so sorry," said Eevie, guiltily looking at the almost-empty bottle. "I almost drank the whole thing."

Tommy smiled back at her, "Eevie, it's fine. We have another bottle and this water," said Tommy, nodding his head down at the lake. "It seems to be extremely clean like an underground spring."

Tommy finished off the last two swigs and was about to fill it with the water from the lake when Eevie grabbed his arm.

"Do you mind swimming out a little farther to get the water? It kind of *creeps* me out that there is a dead, smooshed spider down there."

"Just think of it as a protein smoothie," said Tommy smiling.

Eevie's face scrunched in disgust. "Gross!"

Tommy swam out to the middle of the lake and filled the bottle. The water looked crystal clear, plus he had swallowed plenty of it swimming around. *We'll just drink this if we need to.*

Tommy pulled himself back onto the ledge beside Eevie.

"Eevie, go ahead and eat another power bar. I feel fine," Tommy lied, "and we'll ration the last one if we need to."

Eevie started to say no, but she felt like her blood sugar was low, so she accepted without retaliation.

Grabbing the wrappers, Tommy put them and the Gatorade bottle filled with water into the backpack while Eevie finished her power bar.

"So," said Tommy looking toward the doors. "I guess we swim to the white tunnel, and fingers and toes crossed, it leads us out of here."

Eevie nodded. "I'm ready."

Tommy carefully checked the backpack, making sure it was completely sealed. As he stood, he looked at the deep channels cut into the stone, created by the spider as it dragged itself to the edge of the ledge to launch its final attack on Tommy. Glistening like a black diamond was a razor-sharp hair from the spider's leg embedded in the rock.

Tommy reached down to grab the hair. Instantly, he let out a cry and pulled his hand away. He had barely touched the top yet it had sliced his finger open. He cradled his hand as crimson red blood dripped from his fingertip onto the ledge.

"Are you OK?" asked Eevie, rushing over.

Tommy nodded. "Don't touch that hair!" Tommy held his finger above his heart. The bleeding slowed. It wasn't a deep cut, but enough to remind him that it hurt with every heartbeat.

Tommy dug down into his backpack and pulled out his hoodie, and untied it from Eevie's. He gently wrapped it around the hair to avoid slicing his hands again. Then, placing his hands on either side, he tugged on the hair, rocking his body from side to side.

"Careful, Tommy, you need your hands!"

Tommy didn't reply. He was wary of the hair cutting through his hoodie and into his hand. Cautiously, he continued moving the hair in a circle until finally it broke free from the rock. Tommy victoriously raised the spider hair into the air. It was as light as paper, but felt powerful in his hands. Tommy left it wrapped up in his hoodie and carefully placed it in his backpack.

He turned to Eevie. "Just in case." She nodded, not needing a further explanation.

Tommy swung his arms through his backpack straps and walked with Eevie to the edge of their brief sanctuary, and without another word, they both jumped into the water.

The tunnel wasn't too far away, but as they swam closer, the current grew more and more intense, and the water became frigid. Each stroke and each kick became a fight as the water from the tunnel began to fight back, pushing them back into the lake. By the time they reached the tunnel's entrance, they were exhausted.

"Grab those rocks!" yelled Tommy, pointing to a small shelf of rocks just above the tunnel.

Shaking, Eevie and Tommy pulled themselves onto the small outcrop of rock.

"I feel like I've just gotten a year's worth of cardio in one day," said Tommy.

Eevie just nodded, still fighting to regain her breath and shuddering from the cold.

"It's like American Ninja, only underwater," said Tommy to no one in particular.

"Not helping," said Eevie. "I think we should just rest for a few minutes, and then try again. I don't want to die from hypothermia," she said through chattering teeth.

Tommy nodded and pulled his knees to his chest.

"Maybe the tunnel isn't long, and we can just hang onto the ceiling?" asked Eevie.

"The ceiling is too high above the water level," said Tommy, shaking his head. "I wish Fred could fit; he could power us through the tunnel in no time."

"You mean Fredericka," said Eevie, glancing sideways at Tommy with mock annoyance. "Anything so amazing and awesome has to be a girl—it's pretty much a universal fact."

Tommy was about to reply, but then he smiled.... *She's probably right.* "Are you ready to have another go at it, or are you too busy being amazing?" Tommy playfully shook his friend.

"Let's do it, before I change my mind."

Tommy and Eevie jumped into the water at the mouth of the cave. They gasped as the cold water took their breath away. Immediately, they were blasted backwards by the current. Eevie and Tommy popped to the surface, bobbing like buoys in the rough water.

"This is impossible. We can't fight this current!" yelled Eevie.

"Let's try diving deeper and see if it's any calmer down toward the bottom."

Eevie gave a thumbs-up and they both dove to the bottom of the lake. The current still pushed them back, but they were able to make some progress. Eevie swam up for air, but the water almost completely filled the cave. As she came up, the rushing water flung her against the ceiling and the wall of the cave. Eevie let out a scream as she was spit out of the cave bruised and bleeding. Moments later, Tommy fared the same.

He motioned excitedly for them to return to the rock.

"Did you see it?" asked Tommy excitedly. "Did you see the stones?!"

"See what? What stones?"

"Along the edge of the cave. It's like a sideways ladder. Like someone carved them into the wall of the cave. I think we can hold onto those and use those to pull our way through the water," said Tommy, his voice filled with excitement.

"How far down are they?" asked Eevie. She paused. "Because if they are too far below the surface, unless you can sprout gills, we would have to come up for air and we're just gonna get shot out of the cave again. And I don't think I can take many more whacks to my head," said Eevie, tenderly rubbing a huge throbbing knot on her forehead.

"Eevie, you're a genius!" Tommy exclaimed.

Tommy jumped into the water and reappeared a few moments later with a couple of large reeds.

"Gills," said Tommy proudly. "We'll simply breathe through these." He held out the reeds again for Eevie to see. "That way we don't have to come up to the surface."

Eevie looked doubtful.

"Remind me to cancel your Netflix account when we get back to terra firma."

Tommy ignored her comment.

"We just need to practice before trying it in the tunnel," persisted Tommy. "Do you have a better idea?"

Eevie grabbed a reed from Tommy and jumped into the freezing water. She was right—breathing through the reed wasn't easy.

Water kept going up her nose, and she had to fight back the panicky feeling like she wasn't getting enough air. *This is what it must feel like to be claustrophobic.* But, in the end, she had to agree with Tommy. She wasn't getting a lot of air, but she was able to breathe underwater, and like it or not, this seemed to be the best option.

She swam up. "Tommy, I just thought of something. We have to be able to hang on to the rock wall with one hand when we take a breath. We can't let go to take a breath or we'll get shot out again."

Tommy nodded. She was right. After a half an hour of trial and error, they finally figured out how to hold the reed at a forty-five-degree angle in their mouths with their bottom three fingers. And using their thumb and index finger, they could pinch their nose simultaneously so they didn't inhale water.

"Third time's a charm," said Eevie as they jumped off their perch into the mouth of the cave.

Eevie followed behind Tommy as he dove down about two feet below the surface. Sure enough, she could see them: a series of rock handles that traveled horizontally along the wall in roughly eighteen-inch intervals.

Instead of fighting the current, they let the water pull their bodies almost horizontal as they began their arduous journey.

I'm never eating salmon again, thought Tommy. *Anything that has to fight this hard to survive deserves to live.*

Tommy and Eevie quickly created a pattern to pace themselves. Four stone handles forward, breathe, rest for thirty seconds, repeat. After what seemed like an eternity, Tommy could see a torrent of bubbles and rushing water. It was a waterfall. There was no way around; they would have to try and fight through the deluge of water.

Tommy signaled up with his thumb. He wanted them to get as much air as possible before battling the waterfall. They descended quickly and Tommy grabbed the rock handles with all his might. Water came crashing down onto him, making it impossible to see. *I hope Eevie is OK!*

Ugh! Tommy slammed face first into solid rock. *No, it can't be!*

"Come Closer" – Is Never a Good Thing

Two seconds later, Eevie slammed into the back of Tommy. She looked confusedly at him. A huge boulder was blocking their path. Tommy motioned for Eevie's hand and swam up to the top of the huge boulder. Gripping with all of his might, he looked for a way around the stone. His lungs were screaming, his grip with Eevie was starting to slip, and he knew she needed air. He pushed off hard, and Eevie pulled with all her might to haul him in. That's when he saw it—a channel carved into the wall, hidden by the stone.

He and Eevie quickly kicked, grabbed their reeds, and sucked in much-needed oxygen for a couple of minutes. Tommy fought back fear. He had exhausted himself, and his lungs needed more air than he was able to suck in. *Calm yourself, Tommy. Almost there. Calm yourself.*

Eevie looked worried. There was no way for Tommy to describe what he saw, and he was about to ask her to follow him into a place they may not be able to escape from. He gave her the signal to stay. He wasn't about to have her risk her life for him again.

Tommy wedged himself between the huge boulder and the rock wall. Pushing ferociously, he was able to slowly work his way up to the top of the boulder, and then he was free of the water. He sucked in deep mouthfuls of air. To the right was a hidden series of carved stones leading upward.

Eevie began to shake; the water was freezing. It helped to move, but staying still, her body was beginning to convulse. *Come on, Tommy!*

Just then, she saw Tommy's backpack. She could just make out Tommy's hands, gripping it tightly. *Does he want me to take his backpack? Is he stuck?*

Eevie gripped the backpack only to have it ripped out of her hands. *What is he doing?* her mind screamed.

The backpack reappeared again. This time she grabbed it and hung on. She felt herself being pulled up. Her reed broke loose, and she turned her head to see it immediately crushed in the churning water. Using her legs, she pushed herself while Tommy pulled her to the top of the boulder. With her nose just a few inches from the ceiling, she gulped in air. She was alive, Tommy was alive, and that was all that mattered.

"You made it!" said Tommy breathlessly.

Eevie nodded. "Invitation via backpack officially accepted."

Tommy pointed at the rocky wall. "Those carved rocks go up about 20 feet, and above that...!"

"Light!" said Eevie excitedly.

Eevie didn't wait for a second invitation and began crawling hand over hand up the wall. She could hear Tommy panting as he followed close behind her. A pale, flickering light beckoned Eevie onward. At the top of the stairs, Eevie could see a narrow passage cut through the stone. Cautiously, she pulled her head and shoulders through the opening. She let out an audible gasp.

"What is it?" asked Tommy, clambering up the makeshift steps behind her. Eevie pulled herself the rest of the way through the small opening. Slowly, she turned in a circle, taking in the room.

The room was small and cold and veiled in thick shadows. The air was moldy and heavy, making their eyes burn and water. Flames flickered atop long, thin black candles, sending thick rivulets of melting wax dripping down the ragged stone walls to the floor.

Carved into the walls were hundreds of white faces, their eyes closed as if in prayer. In the center of the room was an altar of sorts, carved out of what looked like white marble. A huge, ragged, leather-bound book lay on top.

"Woh...," said Eevie crossing her arms and shivering. "It's freezing in here."

"More like creepy," whispered Tommy.

"Fine, creepy and cold," agreed Eevie.

Tommy dropped to one knee and opened his backpack. He pulled out Eevie's hoodie and sneakers.

"Thanks," said Eevie through chattering teeth.

Tommy carefully unrolled his favorite hoodie. The razor-sharp hair fell to the ground, making a hollow, metallic ting sound. He held his hoodie up; light shone through the jagged cuts in the fabric. "Great...it looks like Edward Scissorhands is my tailor."

"Don't complain—you have a brand new set of clothes to wear to church."

"Church?" Tommy asked, confused.

"Yes," laughed Eevie, "because they're holy."

"Eev... really?" said Tommy, shaking his head.

"Holy, get it?"

"Yes, can we please move past this awkward moment and focusing on getting out of here?"

"No one is ever going to believe us when we finally get out of here," said Eevie, looking at the faces on the wall. *Did one of the faces open its eyes?* An ice-cold chill ran up her spine and she walked over to Tommy's side. She stared again. It was a face near the bottom, she was sure.

"Can you blame them?" asked Tommy, continuing the conversation and walking toward the altar. "Eevie, check your phone. See if you have any battery left. We can at least take a few pictures as proof."

"Are you sure we want to waste what little battery we have left? What if we get a signal?"

"I hardly think a couple of pictures is going to kill your phone."

Eevie shrugged and grabbed her phone from Tommy's backpack.

"It's at eighteen percent," she said matter-of-factly.

"OK, just take two or three pictures of the room. Like those creepy faces, the old book..."

Eevie turned toward the wall of faces. The flash from her camera blinded them.

"Ah, you scorched my eyes again," said Tommy, watching globs of orange and greenish white light dance across his line of vision.

"Then close your eyes," said Eevie, shaking her head. "I'm going to take one of the book and the altar-looking thing."

Another flash illuminated the room.

"OK, done. We now have proof."

"Eevie, I'm gonna take the book too. Who knows what we'll find inside?"

"I don't know if that's a good idea," said Eevie, shaking her head. "I've seen too many movies about bad things happening to good people when they take something that isn't theirs."

"Eevie," said Tommy seriously, "this book might answer a lot of questions. We have no idea where we are, and why this is happening to us."

"I guess," said Eevie, still hesitant.

Tommy grabbed the book and pulled. It wouldn't budge, as if it was glued to the altar. He tried to open the book; the pages seemed to be sealed together. "What the heck?"

Tommy pulled and pushed from every angle. "Maybe it's not even really a book."

"Maybe we should just leave it alone and keep going."

Tommy looked at her disappointedly. "It could have clues, you know. Did you at least get a picture of it?"

"Yes."

Eevie opened the photos on her phone.

"Here are the faces." She quickly swiped to the next picture. "And here's the book."

They both saw it at once. The flash had made visible what couldn't be seen with the naked eye.

"Eevie, there is something on the cover of the book!"

"I see it. I see it," whispered Eevie excitedly.

"Eevie, take a close-up picture of the book, like right on top of it."

Eevie held her phone directly over the book. "Close your eyes. I don't want to scorch them again," smirked Eevie.

Tommy just stared at her, nodding his head and giving her the "come on, come on" gesture with his hand.

Like lightning, the flash illuminated the room.

Eevie stepped back and opened the picture.

"Whoa," whispered Tommy.

The book cover revealed the word "APERIO," and under that, an outline of a human hand.

"You don't suppose...," whispered Eevie.

"APERIO," said Tommy, directed at the book.

Disappointingly, nothing happened. Eevie placed her hand on the book, on top of the invisible hand on the cover. "APERIO."

Again, nothing.

"Did you use the same hand as in the picture?"

"I think so," said Eevie, opening the image again.

Tommy placed his hand over the invisible hand. "APERIO!"

Suddenly, the serpent's eyes on his ring glowed blood red. He quickly pulled his hand away. The cover flew open. As if by an invisible hand, pages turned to the center of the book.

Tommy couldn't turn away. On the page were two closed eyes and the words "Come Closer."

"Tommy, what is it?"

Tommy's voice caught in his throat. "Two eyes and the words 'Come Closer,'" he whispered hoarsely.

Suddenly the eyes flew open. Tommy screamed, jerking his head back. A face appeared and as if the page were made of stretch silk, the face began to come out of the book. Tommy tried to jump away, but from the altar, two marble hands locked around his wrist.

Tommy twisted and pulled, screaming. The face began whispering, "Come closer."

Eevie screamed, grabbing the book. She tried to close the cover. She tried to pull Tommy away with all her might, but nothing.

She looked for a huge rock to smash the book, and then she saw it, the spider's hair. Rushing over, she picked it up. She grimaced as it cut through her flesh, warm blood running down her fingers. She ran over to the book and with one hand steadying the steely hair and one hand atop, she drove it down into the face. A horrific scream cried out. Tommy ripped his hands free, falling onto the floor. He looked up and all of the eyes on the wall opened.

Eevie grabbed the book. The face was still screaming, black, bloody ink dripping from the face to the ground. The book writhed and fought in her hands. She ripped and tore at the pages. Spinning, she slammed the book against the wall, driving the spider hair completely through the book.

Tommy grabbed the book from her, rushed over to the stone ladder, and threw the book down into the raging waterfall.

Eevie stood shaking, adrenaline coursing through her body. She held her bloody hands against her chest.

"You OK?" asked Tommy, his eyes filled with worry.

"Tommy, those eyes," she said, not wanting to look at the wall.

"Yeah."

"They're watching us."

"I know..." said Tommy angrily.

Inside, he was battling the desire to smash each and every one of those faces into oblivion.

"What do you think that was, Tommy? What do they want from us?"

"I don't know. But I do know one thing. Whoever it was has a massive headache now."

Eevie smiled at her friend. Her heart felt like it added an extra beat now when she looked at him.

"Oh, and I do know one other thing." Tommy was still talking. "You know the saying 'you can't judge a book by its cover'?" Tommy shook his head. "They have no idea."

"None."

The eyes followed their every movement.

Eevie picked up the scraps of paper she had torn from the book. Many of the pages were covered in bloody black ink, but a few of the pages she could see contained a lot of text.

Tommy shuddered when he saw the pages from the book.

"What do they say?"

"I'm not sure," said Eevie. "I can't tell if this is Latin or what language it's written in."

"If we make it out of here, we'll have the pictures and these pages as proof that this awful place exists."

Tommy walked back to the altar. Where the book had been before, a single black stone lay in a hollowed-out depression. Tommy picked up the glistening stone. He looked at the wall of staring faces.

One of the faces stared back with only one eye. Tommy walked toward the face. The face immediately tried to close his eye, but Tommy was too fast. He quickly pushed the black stone into the empty eye socket.

There was a loud grating sound as the wall beside them groaned and shook, revealing a staircase.

"Oh, cool," said Eevie.

Then her expression soured. "It leads down, Tommy; it leads *down.*"

Eevie felt Tommy's hand on her shoulder. Hot tears began to well up in her eyes. She thought about her family, her friends. This seemed more like a horrible nightmare where she was fighting and fighting to wake up, but the dream world had other ideas.

"Eevie! Eevie!" Tommy's voice finally broke through. "The wall is closing! Hurry!"

Tommy pushed Eevie through the opening. A thin slab of rock barely large enough for them to stand on was all that separated them from a series of steps that descended at least a hundred feet into the cave. On either side of them stood solid walls of rock.

Wham! Eevie and Tommy jumped as the wall slammed shut beside them, sending up a cloud of dust and debris.

"Geez," exhaled Tommy, whipping around. "I guess we over-stayed our welcome."

They looked down the narrow stairway; the angle was impossibly steep. The walls were illuminated by thin, black candles that stood like centurions.

"It makes me dizzy just looking down there," said Eevie, peering over the edge.

"We don't really have a choice. We'll just go down slowly and take our time. We can use the walls to balance ourselves," said Tommy reassuringly.

Eevie placed her hand onto the wall and placed her foot onto the first step. She turned slowly to Tommy. "One step down, ninety-nine to..."

Eevie never got to finish her sentence as the step crumbled beneath her. She screamed. Throwing her arms up, she grabbed a candle holder. The candle holder turned downwards, and hot wax poured onto Eevie, searing her hand and wrist. As Eevie screamed out in pain, the candle holder ripped from the wall and Eevie plunged downwards. Throwing out her arms, she clung to the next step as her feet dangled into blackness where the first step had been.

"Tommy!" screamed Eevie as the step crumbled under her fingertips.

I'm Falling for You

Tommy didn't hesitate. He jumped down onto the third step, clawing at the walls so he didn't lose his balance. Eevie's hands were scrambling at the step as it disintegrated, crashing down into the unknown.

Tommy knelt down. His foot slipped to the step below him. It shattered under his weight, falling into nothingness. Tommy regained his balance, then crouched on the tiny step and grabbed Eevie's hands. Placing his back against the wall, he pulled with all his might. Her hands were slippery and wet with sweat. Tommy closed his eyes. He leaned back even more, his body now precariously hovering over empty space where the step had been. The fact that the crumbling steps never seemed to hit the ground did not escape him.

Eevie's hand slipped. Tommy screamed and yanked so hard he thought he might snap her arm out of joint. Half of Eevie's body was now on the step. As if pulling up a bucket using a rope, Tommy worked his way down her arm, pulling her closer and closer onto him, until at last, Eevie lay across his legs and chest.

For a long time, she didn't move. She felt dizzy and sick. Angry, hot tears streamed down her cheeks. Tommy closed his eyes and tried to slow his breathing. They had both narrowly escaped death and he couldn't keep his body from shaking. For now, they seemed safe on a step that was barely wider than Tommy's leg.

After what seemed like an eternity, Eevie looked up at Tommy, her eyes red and swollen. "At least this step held...but who knows about the others."

"I've been thinking about that. Every single puzzle has been set up to move us through this nightmare maze to get to somewhere."

Eevie listened silently.

"Why would they make a stairway that is impossible to get down? They wouldn't," said Tommy, answering his own question. "We just have to figure this out without falling into the eternal abyss of death. So far we know that the first two steps crumbled but this one held. So I suggest we use this step as home base and carefully try to test the other steps."

"I was thinking," said Eevie, wiping the tears from her face with the back of her hand, "that maybe it's some sort of a test. If you make it through the maze, then...hopefully, you're free. But, those who didn't make it through the maze are never heard from again. Does that make sense?"

"Nothing makes sense, Eevie. Honestly, I think that at any moment, I'm going to wake up and all of this will have been a dream. Ouch, what the heck? Why did you pinch me?"

"You're welcome," smiled Eevie. "You're not dreaming."

"Can we please get back to testing my step theory? You're invading my personal space."

Eevie smiled. She needed this. She needed a plan, something to move them forward. Her near-death experience had really shaken her, and it helped to have Tommy take the lead.

Tommy carefully stood as if on a tightrope. He stretched his arms out. He was easily able to touch each wall with his outstretched hands. Keeping one foot on the step and supporting most of his body weight with his hands, he smashed his right foot onto the next step.

Eevie gasped as the step immediately collapsed. Quickly, Tommy brought his foot back to safety. They both listened and listened...nothing.

Eevie's body was beginning to stiffen with fear. Her legs began to tremble with the thought of standing on a step no wider than a pencil, with nothing but blackness on either side of her.

"Eevie, I think I've found the pattern.... If this next step holds, then we'll simply need to choose every third step!"

Eevie nodded her head yes. Now she knew how it felt to be a high-rise construction worker walking across steel girders hundreds of feet in the air. She closed her eyes; just the thought gave her vertigo.

"Eevie, I'm going to test the third step. If it holds, you will need to jump down to me."

Eevie nodded. She watched as Tommy raised his leg and then slammed it into the third step. The shock of slamming into something solid jarred Tommy's leg, causing him to fight for balance.

"OK, I think we've found our pattern," said Tommy matter-of-factly. "I'll run one more test just to be sure when we get to the next step."

Tommy looked at Eevie. He knew she was struggling, so he smiled at her. "Eevie, you and I go up and down steps every day. This isn't going to be any different," he said soothingly.

"Yeah, but if we fall off the steps at home, we don't fall into the abyss. I fall on my shag carpet or my dog."

Tommy tilted his head. "Eevie," he said evenly, "you're not going to fall. I'm not going to let you fall. Put your back against the wall, and slowly stand. Use the wall for support."

Eevie slowly slid up the wall. Her legs felt weak, as if they were going to abandon her at any moment. She stood and got her bearings.

"You got it," encouraged Tommy.

"If you let me fall, I promise you my ghost will haunt you for the rest of your life."

"I'm more frightened of the thought of having to deal with you the rest of my life," laughed Tommy. "OK, Eevie, let's do this." Tommy reached out his hand; Eevie leaned forward and grabbed it tightly. Without warning, she leaped down onto the step with Tommy, slamming him into the wall with a thud, her forehead cracking against his.

"Ugh," Tommy exhaled as stars exploded behind his eyes. "Don't they teach you about concussions in soccer?" he asked, rubbing his head.

Eevie continued holding onto Tommy for a moment. She was feeling better, but unfortunately, as she did the math in her head, they were going to have to repeat this process at least another thirty times.

Nearly an hour later, they could finally see the bottom of the stairs. As they descended, a small room about the size of a tool shed became visible. Directly behind Eevie and Tommy was the staircase of doom. In front of them was a small stone room lit by two candles.

Tommy crouched down on the last remaining step and gasped, "Holy..."

Eevie crouched down beside him, placing her hand on the wall. Before them stood a giant wooden door. There was writing on top of the door, and across the middle of the door were four evenly spaced wooden buttons numbered 2, 3, 4, and 5.

But what caught their attention was the floor. At least a half dozen skeletons lay on the last step and on the floor in front of the door. A dismembered hand and arm hung from the door handle.

"Eevie, remember when you said that you thought that there were some people that made it through and some that didn't? I have a feeling that we are meeting the unlucky ones that didn't make it," said Tommy quietly.

"They made it this far and died...but why?" asked Eevie.

Tommy pointed. "Because of that—another puzzle.... Whoever did this must have been denied books or puzzles as a child, and now they're trying to make up for lost time?"

Eevie ignored Tommy and began reading the puzzle out loud. "If the answer to 6 is 3 and the answer to 12 is 6, what is the answer to 8?"

"Well that's easy—the answer is 4," said Tommy. "Four, right? This is our easiest one yet! Half of 6 is 3, half of 12 is 6, and half of 8 is 4." He stared at Eevie, waiting for her to acknowledge his sudden ability to coax his geek gene into action. And to further prove his point, he pointed at the 4 button. It was worn smooth from being selected more than the others.

Tommy studied her expression and said, "I know what you're thinking. The answer is too obvious, isn't it?"

Eevie shook her head in agreement. "Yes, it's too easy. I think that it's a trap. They want us to believe it's 4, and I'm betting these poor souls picked 4 as well. I need to think this through."

When it came to intuition, Tommy had learned long ago to trust Eevie. If she felt that something was amiss, they should proceed with caution. Right now her "amiss meter" was registering at 100 percent.

He began repeating the riddle over and over in his mind. *If 6 is 3 and 12 is 6, what is 8? Maybe if I spell out the letters in* six, three, twelve, six, *and* eight *and take the first letters—they always do that in mystery books. STTSE. Does that make a word? Ugh, it doesn't matter because I need a number, and those letters don't spell a number.*

He tried arranging the letters in his head, but none of the combinations seemed to even form a word.

Wait. He had another thought. *What if I count the letters in the words?* Six *has three letters,* three *has five letters,* twelve *has six letters,* six *again has three letters, and* eight *has five.*

"So," he whispered to himself, "3, 5, 6, 3, 5." *The next number in the sequence should be 6!*

"Eevie, I think I got it!" said Tommy excitedly. "Listen, before I confuse myself! The numbers in the riddle are 6, 3, 12, 6, and 8. If you count the letters in each number, you get 3, 5, 6, 3, 5.... Do you see the pattern? The next number should be 6!"

"Tommy, there's no 6; it only goes up to 5. But I think you're a genius."

"Of course I'm a genius," said Tommy, giving Eevie a look that said that 'everyone pretty much thinks this—it goes without saying.' "So, while I know that I've provided you with the key information that you need to solve the riddle, tell me what you think I know, and I'll tell you if you're right," said Tommy confidently, folding his arms across his chest.

Shaking her head, Eevie smiled. "I'm not going to even pretend to understand that. Shut up and listen for a second. If this works, I'll buy you a T-shirt that says 'Genius' on it."

Tommy made a zipping motion across his mouth, then whispered, "I wear a men's medium or a boy's husky."

Ignoring him, Eevie began. "Look, if we break the puzzle up, it's really quite simple. If 6 is 3, it means that the number 6 when spelled out has three letters. Then 12 is 6 because when spelled out..." Tommy finished her sentence.

"Twelve has 6 letters!"

"The 8 is 5, Tommy," said Eevie excitedly. "The answer is 5!"

"You're right, that's exactly what I was thinking," smiled Tommy. "We make a great team."

"There's only one problem," said Eevie, staring at the door. Tommy followed Eevie's stare. A skeletal hand and the bony remains of an arm hung from the door handle. The bony hand was clenched in a fist as if the person died trying to pull the door open.

"You're afraid of the skeleton? After all that we've been through, it's a skeleton that stops progress?"

"I'm not afraid of the skeleton," said Eevie. "I just didn't want to have to touch the skeleton...it's creepy."

"Fine, I'll move it. I want to get out of here."

"No, I need to do this," said Eevie.

She pulled on the arm. There was a crisp snap as the arm separated from the hand.

"Ugh." Eevie dropped the arm as an involuntary shiver rose up her spine. "I'm thinking he was low on calcium," she said, arching her eyebrows.

"Perhaps a little less protein in your diet...sheesh," said Tommy.

Eevie grabbed the skeletal hand. *Wow, it's really on there.* She wrapped her hand around the hand and pulled. SNAP! The hand broke free as several bony fingers fell to the ground. Eevie looked at the hand and was about to toss it with the rest of the skeleton when she saw something that gave her chills.

The hand had a serpent ring on it just like Tommy's.

"Tommy," Eevie hissed. "Look!" She held up the bony finger to show Tommy.

"Drop it," Tommy yelled. "Drop it!"

WE'RE NOT ALONE...

Before Eevie could let go, the serpent quickly slithered around her finger. Eevie screamed and tore at the snake. The ring squeezed tighter and tighter. Eevie watched in horror as the serpent's head drew back and drove its fangs into Eevie's finger.

Eevie screamed, tearing and pulling, but the ring wouldn't budge. The snake's fangs turned red with Eevie's blood. She stared transfixed as its silvery eyes turned blood red.

Eevie stared up at Tommy, having forgotten about the ring until now. Now she understood how he must feel to have this horrid thing wrapped around his finger. Her heart beat angrily in her chest. Her finger ached and throbbed.... Tommy wrapped his arms around his friend; he didn't know what to say. The only words that came out were, "I know...I know."

Tommy clenched his jaw and slammed his fist into the number 5. There was a loud metallic click as the door unlocked. He grabbed the handle and yanked the massive door open.

Light poured in from the open doorway, blinding them. A thick, horrid stench filled their lungs, gagging them. Reflexively, they covered their faces with their hands to let their eyes adjust to the light.

They both jumped as the door slammed shut behind them, the sound of the loud metallic click letting them know that the door had locked.

Through watery eyes they took in the room. It was massive, like a cathedral. Scattered throughout the room, thick spiral columns of twisting stone rose up to the ceiling. What looked to be hieroglyphics covered them from top to bottom. Huge gray boulders were scattered across the ground like marbles.

Across the room, a set of stairs ascended into a dark tunnel that cut through the rock. Giant black lanterns lined the walls, illuminating the room, and in the center of the floor lay a huge pile of clothes, shredded and caked with dirt and dark stains that they could only imagine was blood. Bones were scattered throughout the room and up the darkened stairway.

"This is cheery," whispered Tommy through clenched teeth, his eyes darting back and forth.

Eevie slowly turned in a circle, her eyes scanning every detail of the room. Her eyes followed each column toward the ceiling, looking for a hidden ladder or doorway. The only exit she could find was a set of carved stone steps, leading up into yet another dark tunnel.

While Eevie searched for a way out, Tommy investigated the huge boulders. He wanted to make sure there weren't any un-wanted, hidden surprises. As he walked toward the pile of clothes, the stench was incredible, his throat burning with each breath.

"Eevie, some of these clothes look like they are centuries old." He picked up a tattered wool jacket. A gold locket fell from one of the pockets to the ground.

Tommy held it up by the chain. It was a beautiful gold locket with ornate patterns inlaid in the gold. "Whoa, Eevie, check out this locket—it's beautiful!"

Eevie ran over to Tommy. "Let me see."

She turned the locket over in her hands. She pushed on a pin that protruded slightly from the bottom and it popped open. Inside was a small piece of folded parchment.

"Tommy, look," said Eevie excitedly. "There's a piece of pa-per inside."

Eevie carefully unfolded the yellowed paper.

"It looks like it's Latin," said Tommy, leaning over her shoulder.

"*Incantamentum*," whispered Eevie. "Maybe like an incantation? Like magic?"

"What does it say under that?" asked Tommy. "Anything in good old English?"

"It says, '*Inprecor—Invoko Presamis Ignis Potionem (duo),*'" said Eevie, slowly trying to say each word. "Tommy, the top must mean something like an incantation and then the word *Invoko* must mean to invoke whatever the rest of this means.

"Well," pointed out Tommy, "the word *duo* has to mean two. So...does that mean you say it together, or you say it twice?"

"Maybe we should look at the World Translate app. I don't know if we should be saying something when we have no idea what we're saying."

"If you turn into a frog, I'm sorry but I'm not going to kiss you," said Tommy, smiling.

"Good idea. I'll get you that genius T-shirt in matching colors if you keep this up."

Eevie grabbed her phone. Her fingers flew across the screen as she loaded the translator app.

"The first word, *Inprecor*, means a wish or a curse. I was right, *Invoko* means to invoke. Hmm, that's strange, *Presamis* isn't recognized by any of the language dictionaries." She looked at the writing again: *P-r-e-s-a-m-i-s*. She hit enter again; no match.

"Just skip that word, Eevie. What are the other ones?"

"*Ignis* means, uhm...torch or fire."

"Oh yeah, like ignite," interrupted Tommy.

Eevie nodded. "And *Potionem* means..."

"Potion, I bet," said Tommy, nodding his head. "Right? Man, I got this Latin thing down! I should have taken Latin, not Spanish. I'm a natural."

Eevie sighed. "Yes and yes, and you're right, *duo* means two."

"So," said Tommy, puffing up his chest and speaking in his most authoritative voice, "this is a curse, and you make it happen by saying those words. I still don't get it. Is it a fire potion? Because that makes absolutely no sense."

"There's another curse below it, *Inprecor*, which we know means curse." Then Eevie sounded out the next word. "*Vene-fi-cium*, which means..." She paused as she typed. "Poison, and *tango* means...touch.... So...Poison touch! So sinister..." Eevie raised her eyes from her phone and noticed Tommy was no longer joking.

"Eevie, don't look up," whispered Tommy out the side of his mouth. "We're not alone."

"Wha..." The look on Tommy's face stopped her.

The hair stood up on the back of her neck as she felt the slow, icy crawl of panic move up her spine. She carefully followed his eyes. It took her a minute to see it. Mixed within the hieroglyphics was a strange-looking monkey creature. Like a chameleon, the creature had taken on the color of the column, and the hieroglyphics appeared on its body as a strange living camouflage, giving the appearance that it was transparent.

"It looks like a really strange monkey," whispered Eevie.

Peeling itself slowly from its perch, the animal turned and stared directly at Eevie and Tommy, and then without warning let out a screaming shriek that turned their blood to ice.

Without thinking, Tommy grabbed Eevie by the arms and pulled her behind the nearest boulder. Scrambling in the dirt, he picked up a baseball-sized stone, and then peered around the boulder. The creature let out another shrill scream and then leapt up onto the column just a few feet from where they were hiding.

"Go away! Go away!" shouted Tommy, raising the huge rock threateningly.

The beast turned its head and scowled at Tommy, baring its razor-sharp canines.

Tommy gulped. The monkey had incredibly large claws that left claw marks in the rock as it moved. He felt around on the ground for another rock, just in case he missed with the first one.

Suddenly, the monkey let out a howl that reverberated off the walls, causing Tommy and Eevie to clutch their hands over their ears.

Tommy watched as the creature quickly scampered across the ground, up the stairs, and into the mouth of the tunnel. It turned, baring its teeth at Tommy as if daring him to follow it.

"I'm not afraid of you!" yelled Tommy, lying. Inside, his heart was pounding, and he could feel his hands shaking.

Eevie was peering around the other side of the rock. She looked up at Tommy. "I bet we have to go up those stairs to get out of here, and that creature knows it."

"Who knows how many of those things there could be?" said Tommy. "We could be walking into an ambush."

Eevie picked up a couple of smaller stones. She filled the pockets of her hoodie to the point she was afraid it would rip. She looked at Tommy, who was filling his pockets as well. *We either continue, or we die, and I don't want to die.*

"That thing is crazy fast, and it has massive teeth and claws," said Tommy, emphasizing *teeth* and *claws*.

Darting from the boulder, they reached the bottom of the steps.

"Do you think they are a trap like the other stairs?" asked Eevie, nervously.

"I don't think so. The monkey creature ran up the steps and he looks like he weighs at least fifty pounds. But...to be safe...." Tommy paused, thinking. "Let's go single file, just in case. So we're not standing on the same step."

The monkey had disappeared from the entrance of the cave. The inside of the cave was dark, lit by a few sparsely placed lanterns. The interior was much larger than they had thought, and to their right an underwater stream ran beside them and disappeared into a large crack at the entrance of the cave.

The tunnel looked as if it had been hand chiseled. Deep grooves remained where tools had bitten into the rock. To their left, jagged outcrops of rock lined their path.

Eevie grabbed Tommy's arm.

"What?" whispered Tommy.

She pointed to the wall. Written on the wall was the word *Mortus.*

Underneath were dozens of names: Eli, Sara, Christopher, Edward, Elizabeth.... "Does *mortus* mean dead, like *mortem?*" whispered Tommy.

Eevie nodded. "I'm pretty sure it does."

"There's like a hundred names. Who would kill all of these people?" whispered Tommy, not expecting a reply.

Eevie froze as a few of the names began to fade in and out. The black outline became clear. It was the monkey.

"Tommy!" screamed Eevie.

The monkey jumped from the wall to a row of rocks on their left. He let out a horrific screech that made their ears ring. Both Eevie and Tommy reached into their hoodies and pulled out their rocks.

"Eevie, back up slowly. We have a better chance fighting it in the open space."

The monkey jumped from the stone to the ground. It began moving toward them more rapidly, its claws digging into the rocky soil. Tommy threw a rock as hard as he could. The monkey was fast, but the jagged rock hit the monkey in the chest. The monkey screamed out in pain, as Tommy grasped another rock, daring the monkey to come closer.

The monkey scampered up to the ceiling above their heads, making it very difficult to throw a rock at it with any precision. It clawed at the rock above their heads, and stone and dirt fell into their eyes.

Suddenly, the monkey jumped from the ceiling onto Eevie's back. She screamed as its claws dug into her shoulders. Tommy grabbed two stones and smashed them together on both of the monkey's temples. The monkey dropped to the ground. Screaming in pain, it grabbed Eevie's leg and bit, driving its canines into her calf.

Eevie screamed and fell to the ground. Tommy kicked the monkey, driving it off Eevie and into the water. Eevie lay on the ground, writhing in pain, grabbing her leg.

"Eevie, hang on—I'm gonna get you out of here." The monkey began to crawl out of the water. "Oh no you don't," growled Tommy.

"Tommy...so much hatred, so much anger," said a strained, whispering voice inside his head.

"Who said that?" screamed Tommy, whipping his head side to side.

"Deathhhh." The voice gurgled and bubbled in his brain. It sounded like someone drowning.

A huge creature appeared. Tommy couldn't figure out if it was floating or standing. It had black and gray tattered clothes that seemed to swirl and move around its body. Its face was long and skull-like; loose flesh hung as if melted by a candle. Black, meaty eye sockets were empty, and its mouth was a flesh circle filled with rows of spiky teeth that went all the way around. Black drool spilled down the creature's mouth onto its chest. Each breath made a disgusting, airy, gurgling sound.

The monkey, battered and bloody, dragged itself over to him.

"Whatttt have youuuu donnnnne, you foooooools?" From the swirling fabric, a bony hand appeared. The creature rested its hand on the monkey. "Emaculo," he whispered.

The monkey's injuries healed before their eyes. *Magic*, thought Eevie to herself. *He's using magic.* Tommy turned back to Eevie. She had dragged herself to his backpack. A dark red streak of blood marked her path. She was desperately digging inside for something. She dumped the contents onto the ground.

"Eevie, what are you doing?!" screamed Tommy.

"*Inprecor—Invoko Presamis Ignis Potionem!*" she screamed. "*Inprecor—Invoko Presamis Ignis Potionem!*"

Nothing happened.

"*Inprecor—Invoko Presamis Ignis Potionem, Inprecor—Invoko Presamis Ignis Potionem!*"

The creature laughed, spraying black spittle. "Foolish girl! Do you think that you are a chosen one? That you can just speak the words of an ancient spell and they will work for you?"

Eevie looked down at the water bottle. It was hidden from view behind the backpack, but something *was* happening inside the bottle. It had turned red and it was bubbling. She touched the bottle; the plastic was now melting.

The creature laughed and pointed at Tommy. "Kill him!"

I KNOW YOU CAN HEAR ME...

Tommy threw a rock at the monkey, but it missed and struck the creature. Tommy backpedaled and grasped another rock.

"Tommy," screamed Eevie, "move!" He looked up just in time to see Eevie hurl a red, glowing object at the monkey. The water bottle landed at the monkey's feet and exploded, sending red liquid over its body. The monkey screamed, and then right before their eyes, it melted into nothingness.

"Whoa!" yelled Tommy, jumping back.

"Fooool!" screamed the creature. Black spittle sprayed from his mouth, running in rivulets down his chest.

"Disgusting!" Tommy rushed to Eevie's side. "Can you stand?"

The creature, which seemed to be unable to see them, stretched out its thin, bony hands.

"Don't worry about your friend," he hissed. "You killed Lumous. Now your friend will be my prisoner; her eyes will become my eyes."

Tommy watched in horror as the creature opened its mouth. Black liquid spewed out onto the ground and began racing toward Eevie.

Eevie screamed, and in a fraction of a second her feet were covered with the shiny black liquid. Eevie's body began to convulse as the liquid began to go into her skin, into her veins. Her head began thrashing back and forth and tears streamed from her eyes.

Tommy reached down and tried pulling her away, but she seemed to be cemented in place. Reaching in his pocket he grabbed a large, jagged rock and hurled it at the monster. Thud! The rock hit the creature's forehead, and black blood flowed down its face from the gash.

The monster staggered backwards. *He can't see! The monkey was his eyes. That's what he meant by using Eevie's eyes!*

"Eevie," screamed Tommy, "I'm going to get you out of here! Keep fighting!"

In her mind, she told Tommy OK. But her body, her face, her lips were paralyzed. All Tommy could see were her eyes staring up at him.

The creature recovered quickly, too quickly. Like a nightmare, he slowly moved toward them. Tommy felt like he was moving in slow motion.

He pulled on Eevie with every ounce of strength within him. He grimaced and bared his teeth in anger. He felt helpless as he watched the black liquid oozing through her veins to her neck. *That black liquid is his connection to her. It's like he is pouring his soul into her!*

The monster's shadow descended upon Tommy like a misty black fog. The monster laughed; he was inches away from Eevie's feet. Suddenly, Eevie's head whipped to the side, her eyes wide open.

"There you are," whispered the monster.

Eevie willed with everything inside of her to close her eyes, but she was losing herself. Her mind was becoming numb, and a voice was now whispering inside of her. "Wake up, Eevie," it whispered. "Wake up."

"Why are you doing this?!" screamed Tommy. "What do you want from us?"

"I want your soul, and then I want to eat everything that's left."

Tommy grabbed Eevie's wrist and tried pulling again. He noticed something in Eevie's fist. He pried open her fingers. *It's the page with the spells!* In desperation, he took a step back and screamed the second curse.

"*Veneficium Tango Autem Mors Entantus Mortiforum!* Agh!!!!"

Lightning rushed through Tommy's veins to his hands; his fingertips turned to fire.

"Agh!" screamed Tommy in pain. His veins felt as if they were filled with molten lava.

"The poison touch!" He ran to the creature and thrust both of his hands into the monster's chest. It let out a bellowing howl. Tommy felt the creature's hands around his wrist, and the black liquid began to pour from the monster's hands into Tommy's arms.

"No!" screamed Tommy, his knees buckling. Fiery tears burned channels into his flesh, blistering his lips. "Your friend is dying, boy. Are you going to let your anger for me kill her?"

"LIAR!" screamed Tommy. He slammed his hands onto the monster's head and squeezed. "LIAR!" Fire rushed out of the empty sockets of the monster's eyes, out of his mouth. The monster's chest began to glow red through its pale, translucent skin.

Tommy's arms shook as he squeezed his hands together with all his might. An ungodly scream erupted from the monster. The monster collapsed to the ground at Tommy's feet. He choked on the black acrid smoke rising from its body.

Tommy took a step back and threw up. A trembling bony finger moved from within its sleeve and touched the ground. A thin black liquid line slowly made its way to the creek. The monster stopped breathing. He was dead.

Tommy rushed over to Eevie. Her body was returning to normal. The black liquid pooled from her body and then started moving toward the creek. Her natural color was returning to her face and lips.

"What, what happened?" Eevie whispered, taking Tommy's hand in hers.

"He's dead, Eevie. He's dead."

Eevie lay her head back to the ground and stared up at the top of the cave. Her eyes met his.

"Tommy what happened to you, your face?" Tommy knew it was bad. He had felt the acid tears searing into his flesh. He had felt the blisters on his lips.

"Is it bad?"

Eevie's eyes filled with tears. "It's the most beautiful thing I've ever seen," she said, touching his face with her hand. "It'll add character to our wedding photos." She smiled, winking at him.

Even though Eevie had been his best friend since childhood, he felt himself blushing.

Eevie shook her head. "All of this because of one boy's report about a tree that tried to swallow him." She looked at Tommy and smiled. "At least there will be no more names added to that wall."

Tommy nodded. "Are you OK to move? I think we should be able to follow this stream; hopefully it leads us out of here."

Eevie nodded. "That sounds like a plan. The monkey bite hurts like you wouldn't believe."

Using the wall and with Tommy's help, Eevie slowly got to her feet. She winced as she tried to put weight onto her leg.

"First my knee, and now my calf," she said. "Good thing I still have my looks."

Tommy pretended to gag. He began grabbing everything and putting it back into the backpack. He groaned as he bent over. Every single muscle ached.

Suddenly there was a rumble. Then everything went wrong. The black liquid had reached the water. They watched in horror as the liquid made its way into the stream and, as the current carried it, the water began to solidify into spiky rocks. The entire cave began to shake, cracks like bolts of lightning formed across the ceiling, and the floor began to disintegrate beneath their feet.

"Run!" screamed Tommy.

Eevie ran as fast as she could, even though the pain in her leg was excruciating. A huge rock fell from the ceiling, striking

Tommy on the shoulder. He shook his head. Stars danced in his vision. Another huge rock fell and shattered at his feet.

Eevie grabbed him by the arm. "Tommy, go!"

Behind them, the cave was collapsing; beside them, the stream was quickly becoming a solid sheet of spiky rock. They raced around a corner and slammed into a huge stone wall. "Tommy!" screamed Eevie. "There's no way out!"

Spinning around, they watched as their world collapsed around them.

Tommy looked at the water.

"Eevie, the water is our only way out!" Eevie didn't hesitate and with her next step, she dove into the water.

Tommy looked over his shoulder as they swam. The monster's inky black magic flowed through the water, turning everything it touched to stone. Beneath them, they watched the ground rip apart as if two giant hands were shredding a piece of cloth. Jagged rocks thrust upward just below Tommy and Eevie.

The ceiling rained rocks and debris down on them as they swam. Dust filled the air, making it impossible to see and breathe.

They dove deeper to avoid being crushed as the ceiling collapsed. Suddenly, they found themselves in a very narrow tunnel; they barely had room to swim side by side.

Tommy looked at Eevie, his lungs burning. She motioned to her mouth. *I know, Eevie, I'm almost out of air too.*

Just then, they saw light. Eevie looked at him and nodded.

Tommy shook his head; he was out of air. He crashed up through the water's surface. Dazzling sunlight hit his eyes. Eevie's head exploded upwards as she gasped for air. The light was incredibly intense. For a few moments, they floated and tried to catch their breath.

When they could finally see, they realized where they were: Whitman's Lake, in Black Hallow Park.

"We made it!" screamed Eevie. "We made it!" Tears streamed down her face as she grabbed Tommy's shoulder.

They both looked skyward as the October sunlight cut ribbons through the clouds. Eevie closed her eyes and breathed in deeply— she was finally home.

Tommy and Eevie swam to the water's edge. Wet and numb, they dragged themselves to the shore. They could hear the thumping rotors of an approaching helicopter. They turned and looked at each other, knowing that it was searching for them.

Eevie stared at Tommy. His face was covered with scrapes and cuts, and his hoodie was soaking wet and shredded. His hands and arms were a crisscross of cuts and bruises. Her own pants were torn, and fresh new blood from the monkey's bite began to bleed through her pant leg.

"We are *so dead*," said Eevie, shaking her head. The stabbing pain in her calf made her grimace with each step.

Tommy reached out and grabbed Eevie's hand in his. "We made it, though." He gave Eevie's hand a squeeze.

The helicopter was now circling above them. In the distance, they could see people running their way. Eevie's dad broke from the pack, racing toward them. Emotion welled up inside of Eevie and tears flooded her face. She began to run toward her dad.

Police, rescue workers, friends, and family surrounded them. The world seemed to be spinning in slow motion, and in the midst of it all, they both heard a voice inside their heads.

"I know where you've been.... I know you can hear me."

Tommy and Eevie's eyes locked in chilling bewilderment.

Through the chaos, one lone figure stood staring at them. He smiled and crossed his arms. His serpent ring glistened in the sunlight. The entirety of his eyes turned black. The ranger casually put on his sunglasses and once again whispered inside their heads.

"I'm coming for you."

Quest Map

Thank you for reading Quest Chasers - The Deadly Cavern!

If you loved the book, please leave us a review on Goodreads, Amazon, Barnes & Noble, Kobo or Apple iTunes/iBooks. We'd love to hear from you! Thank you so much for your help, we are in-credibly grateful!

Sign up for the latest info on upcoming books, bonus content, and free giveaways at questchasers.com

Quest Chasers - The Screaming Mummy will be released Fall 2017!

Printed in Great Britain
by Amazon